Bride on the Run

Milan Watson

To all the families I call my own, by birth,
by marriage and by friendship.

Thank you for your support, encouragement and love. Although we are a dysfunctional bunch, love and loyalty remains.

Also by Milan Watson

Seduced by the Boss

A Stranger Like You (a short story)

Unexpected Mistletoe Kisses (a Christmas Novella)

Sullivan Family Series

Bride on the Run (Book 1)

For Justice or Love (Book 2)

Chapter 1

THE dress was stifling. The undergarment stuck to her body like a second skin. The temperature didn't help. It was the last heat wave of summer; this amount of layers should be outlawed in summer, she thought.

The car wouldn't go fast enough. She had to get away. She felt sweat trickle down from the mass of golden curls that were expertly piled on her head; held there by bobby pins and copious amounts of hairspray; which in itself was a fire hazard.

She only needed to get to the next town. She had a plan; the first part of it was going to be humiliating, but at least she had a plan. Her *own* plan. Luckily she had the forethought to fill the tank with gas yesterday; otherwise her impromptu strategy wouldn't have worked out so well. She'd been driving for four hours; she was hungry, uncomfortable and tired of the curious stares aimed her way from others on the highway.

A sign indicated Wilmington was only ten miles away; this would be her first stop. As she cruised into town she spotted a secondhand car dealer and, drawing in a deep breath, she pulled up. This would be the humiliating part.

As she opened the door she could smell the freshness of a sea breeze. It smelt different in Wilmington than it did in Savannah. Somehow it was not as stifling. She started by tugging out the dress, then shifting her legs out, and finally she stood. Stares were directed her way from passersby, curious and amused. She reached into the cubbyhole for her purse and closed the door, ignoring the onlookers. As she turned around a salesman approached her.

"Can I help you, ma'am?"

The man was in his late forties, with a balding patch and tufts of brown hair sticking out from behind his ears. She could immediately tell the suit was thrift store, but he seemed kind. She needed kind right now.

"Yes, please. I'd like to sell you my car at a reasonable price, and take one of these," and she waved her hand indicating to the budget range of sedans in the lot, "off your hands."

"Is something wrong with your car, ma'am?" he asked, concerned.

"No, nothing is wrong, I simply need something less …" Her voice trailed off. How did she explain this without offending the cars he sold? "Something simpler."

"Certainly. You can call me Hank." He held out his hand, and offered her a friendly smile.

"Sarah Rothman." She shook his hand. It was firm and soft.

Bride on the Run

As he led her into his office, she was glad he hadn't yet mentioned her attire, or questioned her request. His office was small, and smelt of stale coffee, doughnuts and lemon polish.

He indicated where she could have a seat, and went to sit behind an old scuffed desk. On it were pictures of two teenagers, a girl and a boy, and a middle-aged woman. Sarah took this to be his wife and children. Somehow she felt comfortable with this stranger; she took a deep breath, knowing she wanted to explain her decision to him.

"You must be wondering why I'm wearing a wedding dress." She gave a cynical laugh.

Hank smiled kindly. "Well, the thought has crossed my mind, but I thought you'd tell me when you were ready. I guess you're ready now?"

"If I didn't get in my car and start driving four hours ago, I would've been Mrs. Elliot by now. But somewhere between getting my hair done and putting on this dress, I realized that's not what I want." She folded her hands in her lap and looked down at her perfectly manicured nails.

"Couldn't you just explain that to the groom?" Hank enquired.

"Yes, yes I could. But the problem isn't the groom, it's our parents, as this is more a merger of two families than a love match, and they wouldn't listen to reason. So I need to disappear for a while until they realize this wedding isn't going to happen." It felt good, Sarah thought. Saying it out loud didn't make her feel so horrible for leaving without explaining it to Grant. She knew deep down he felt the same. Boxed into a corner with no other choice.

Hank nodded, and didn't voice an opinion; he could see from the determination in her blue eyes she would've ignored his views, so he decided to rather help her. "So how can I help you disappear?"

"I can't use any of my credit cards, or my father will track me down. He's good at finding people. The car outside is paid for. If you can buy it from me at a reasonable price, I can buy something cheaper yet reliable and still have enough money left to get by for a few months." Sarah started fiddling with her watch; what if Hank didn't want to buy the car?

"Well, we don't normally purchase Porsches ..." His gaze went past her to the fire engine red Porsche Cayman GTS looking very out of place in his lot. "There isn't really a market in Wilmington to re-sell them, but let me make a couple of calls and see what I can do. Would you like to maybe get out of that dress while I do that?"

"I'd love to, but as I left in a hurry I have nothing with me except my purse." An ironic smile crossed her face.

"My daughter left her bag here this morning on her way to the mall. She's going to a sleepover tonight." Hank looked Sarah up and down. "You look about her size; see if you can't find something in there."

Hank reached under the table and passed Sarah a flowery tote.

"But what about your daughter? What will you tell her?"

"Don't worry about her, she has enough clothes to clothe half of Wilmington, go on now." He pushed the bag into Sarah's waiting hands. "You'll find a ladies room around the corner."

She thanked him and made her way there, clutching the tote to her chest. Entering the ladies room, she found an empty cubicle and she set it down, catching sight of herself in the mirror.

Bright blue eyes looked back at her, framed with a few of the golden curls that escaped the pins. The bulk of her hair was taken up and decorated with little blooms of baby breath.

The dress, which she didn't choose herself, fit her perfectly. She had never been extremely thin, but had always been comfortable with her curves. The dress was strapless and the bodice clung to her breasts, accentuating their size. It clocked out from the waist down to form a beautiful silhouette. Though it was wrinkled from the driving, it was still brand new. She decided to keep it; she might be able to sell it later if she needed more money.

Sarah found a pair of skinny jeans, a Daytona t-shirt and a grey hoodie in the duffel bag. She barely spared a second glance for the sexy lingerie or the short mini skirt in the bag; obviously Hank's daughter had more than a sleepover planned. She smiled to herself as she dressed.

Amazingly it fit. The t-shirt clung to her skin, she would need to get another one soon, but she simply slipped the hoodie on and zipped it up. She poked about in the bag for shoes, and found a pair of sneakers a size too big but better than the high heels. Bundling up her wedding dress and the three inch heels, she grabbed the tote and headed back to Hank's office.

When she entered, Hank was still on a call. She carefully placed the bag next to his table, and put her dress in the chair and looked at Hank expectantly.

He indicated she could sit in the other chair while he finished up.

After a few minutes Hank hung up the phone, scribbled something on a piece of paper and handed it to her. "That is what I can give you for your car. I know it's a lot less than what you originally paid for it two years ago, but that's the best deal I can find today."

Sarah looked down at the piece of paper, looking completely baffled.

"But ..."

"As I said," Hank explained, "we don't normally acquire these types of luxury vehicles. I have a friend out of state that does. So he said I can buy it on his behalf and he'll wire you the money tomorrow morning. I know you said cash, so I asked him to wire the money directly to me, and then you can pick it up in cash in the morning?" He looked at her expectantly, waiting for an indication of her thoughts regarding his suggestion.

Sarah stared at the piece of paper he handed her, dumbfounded by the amount, when she realized he was waiting for her to speak. "Hank, thank you for your trouble. And of course I understand this is the best you can do. It's more than I expected. I'll take it!"

Hank smiled and offered his hand to seal the deal. "So what do you say we go pick out one of those reliable babies I've got on the floor out there?"

Sarah laughed and followed him outside. After much consideration, and debating options, she decided on a nondescript grey sedan. Hank promised her it was reliable and if it gave her any troubles in the following six months, he would gladly pay for repairs.

After signing the paperwork, he offered the keys.

"You can't give me the keys, Hank, I haven't even paid yet."

"Don't worry, you'll be a flush woman in the morning," Hank laughed. "Anyway, I didn't think you'd like to spend a night in Wilmington driving around in that conspicuous monstrosity you have."

At Hank's description of her car, Sarah couldn't help but laugh as well. "Of course not. Thank you." She took the keys from him and picked up her purse. "Hank, can I ask one last favor of you?" Sarah looked at him questioningly. "Could you maybe borrow me money for a motel for tonight?"

Hank reached into his back pocket, and handed her some notes.

"Here you go, little lady. You can find a decent motel not too far up the road on the left. Come by tomorrow around nine a.m., and we'll get you on your way."

Sarah thanked him and walked towards her new grey sedan. As she climbed behind the steering wheel, she felt as if she was finally in control of her own life.

Chapter 2

THE following morning Sarah woke up disoriented. It took her a few minutes to realize where she was, and why she was there. She then took a quick shower and dressed in Hank's daughter's clothes again; her only other option was the wedding gown.

There was some cash left over after paying for the motel and she decided to stop by thrift store on her way to Hank. She needed another pair of jeans and a few shirts and clean underwear. As soon as the paperwork was sorted this morning, she wanted to stay on the road for as long as possible, putting as much distance between herself and her former life.

She met Hank at the exact time agreed to, and swiftly signed the agreement. Hank gave her a briefcase with the cash inside for her car, then handed her an invoice for the grey sedan.

"That can't be right," Sarah queried. "This is much less than the price that was on the hood yesterday afternoon."

"It's not that much less, and I acquired her for a bargain. I think you're going to need that money if you're planning on disappearing for some time.

"Thank you, Hank, but you've been more than kind enough." Sarah counted off the bills she owed for the car, paying the hood price and the loan, and gave him a few hundred more.

"What's this for?" Hank asked, surprised. "That money's not going to get you far, if you give it away so freely."

"You've helped me; you lent money to a stranger, gave her your daughter's clothes, and paid all the bank fees on drawing this amount of cash. It's only fair."

Hank saw her determination and realized there was no quibbling over her decision. He took her hands in his. "Thank you." Tonight he would take his wife out to the new Steak Ranch in town.

"It's a pleasure. I'll be on my way now and remember to thank your daughter for me."

"Will do. Just one favor I ask of you. Try and come back someday to tell me how it all turned out."

Sarah smiled and promised to do just that. She climbed behind the wheel of the grey sedan and started driving. Without forethought of where she was going, she headed north.

It was past midnight; Sarah was bone tired and promised herself she would halt in the next town. She had been driving all day and only stopped twice for gas and food.

After she crossed the Vermont state line and started taking to smaller roads, she ceased noticing where she was. She was now either in New Hampshire or Maine. Either way, she was stopping.

There was only a little USA left north of her, and the plan was to put distance between herself and Savannah, not to leave the country. A sign welcomed her to Blue Hill. She had never heard of the little town before.

Somewhere she had to find somewhere to sleep. As she drove into town, there was a diner still open. Its neon lights flashed invitingly, even if the 'O' was out and it flashed 'PEN'.

She came to a stop and climbed from her sedan. Her body was sore from sitting all day cooped up behind a steering wheel. She took her time stretching, fully extending her legs and back; both were stiff and strained.

As she walked into the diner she noticed a tray full of apple pie on the counter. She debated on ordering two or three slices when a voice piped up behind her, "Hello! What can I get you? Kitchen's closed but coffee's on."

Sarah turned to find a waitress smiling as she held a pot of coffee. She almost drooled.

"Yes please," she all but pleaded.

The waitress reached over the counter for a cup and handed it to Sarah after filling up.

"Are you expecting someone?" she asked, no doubt finding it odd that a woman would arrive alone at a diner so late at night.

"No, I just came into town." Sarah took a large gulp of coffee. "I hoped someone here would be able to tell me where I can find a motel for the night."

"Oh dear," the waitress replied. "I'm Macie, honey. It seems to me you have a bit of problem. We have some or other convention going on in town this weekend, everything's booked up."

Sarah felt her courage slip. "Great, that's just great." She couldn't stop the words that started tumbling from her mouth. "I've driven all day just to decide to stop in the one town where there isn't lodging for me. Just great!" She swallowed the last of her coffee and handed the cup back to Macie. "How far till the next town?"

"Honey, you have some more coffee, I'll be right back." Macie filled her up and, remembering how she had looked at the pie, placed two pieces in a plate and shoved it in front of Sarah.

She then disappeared into a door, with a sign indicating 'STAFF ONLY'.

Sarah didn't know if Macie felt sorry for her or if she wanted to get away from the crazy lady with verbal diarrhea; either way, she started eating her pie.

A few minutes later Macie came back smiling.

"I just spoke to Gladys. She's a friend of mine that owns Oak Cottages out at Peter's Point. She said a couple of the guys that were staying there had to return to New York on urgent business earlier this evening. She has a bed for you, you can head on over."

She explained how to get to Oak Cottages, and ten minutes later Sarah was back in her car; heading down a very dark road to Peter's Point.

She knocked on the door of Oak Cottages just before one a.m., hearing waves crashing against the rocks down by the beach. The sea breeze was cool and refreshing after a long hot day on the road. Sarah wondered vaguely what the view would be like in daylight.

When Gladys opened the front door to her she was relieved to have found a place to spend the night.

The woman noticed her tired eyes and weary movements. "Welcome, dear, I take it you're Sarah?" Sarah nodded in agreement. "Well then, let me show you to your room. We can sort out the paperwork in the morning; you're half dead on your feet already."

Gladys led her up the stairs to a bedroom on the first floor. She wished Sarah a goodnight and firmly closed the door behind her. Sarah placed the briefcase of money and her purse on the small writing desk. She headed to the bed, promising herself a little lie down before taking a shower. Exhausted, her eyes fell closed as soon as her head hit the pillows.

Sarah woke from the sun's rays through the window playing on her skin. In her weary state she hadn't even thought to close the curtains.

She tried to remember where she was, but foggy sleep still haunted her mind. She gradually drifted awake and the past two days flashed through her mind like a slide show.

Running out on her wedding, selling her car, driving all day and most of the night and ending up in Blue Hill, Maine. A smile slowly teased at the corners of her life. Pride. That was what she felt. She had walked out on everything and everyone she knew, and she had never felt more happy or proud of herself. In the last forty-eight hours she had shaken off all the expectations and responsibilities of being a Rothman and, for the first time, she could just be.

She could feel the cool autumn chill on the morning air and loved the freshness it brought. Slowly getting up, she sauntered over to the window.

The view took her breath away. Oak Cottages was built on an outcrop of land, overlooking the Mount Desert Narrows. Gulls cried in the distance, and she saw little boats bobbing on the sea. She smiled to herself, thinking about staying in Blue Hill.

After a leisurely shower, she strolled downstairs and followed the scents of bacon frying, soon finding herself in a large farm style kitchen. Gladys was at the stove, juggling several pans with a juicer buzzing behind her.

"Good morning," Sarah greeted her.

Gladys turned around, and Sarah felt as if she was meeting the woman for the first time. She had a vague recollection of arriving last night, and being welcomed and shown to her room by a kind lady before she passed out. Gladys reminded Sarah of everyone's favorite aunt. Her auburn hair had a soft curl and just touched her shoulders. She wasn't overweight at all, but the few extra pounds she carried gave her an aura of comfort and softness. Her eyes were a doe brown with a few lines etched there from smiling.

She smiled at Sarah with a pan in hand. "Hello, sleepy head. You sleep well? Looked like you needed it last night when you arrived."

"Yes, thank you. I was driving all day yesterday. I think if that kind lady at the diner hadn't called you, I would've been happy to sleep in one of the chairs right there." Feeling at home, she closed in to the stove to peer over Gladys's shoulder. "That looks amazing!"

On the gas burner there were a variety of pans, all sizzling away with bacon, mushrooms, fried tomatoes, eggs, sausages and what looked to be bananas frying in syrup.

Gladys let out a deep sigh.

"I'm sorry I can't be a better hostess this morning, but I have twenty-six people that will be in for breakfast in thirty minutes and Lila just phoned in sick, again! There is coffee in the dining room; you go enjoy some of that, and I'll have breakfast ready in jiffy." Gladys quickly flipped the strips of bacon to allow the other side to fry.

Mumbling in a softer tone she went on, "It's high time I find someone more reliable to help out around here."

Sarah had always enjoyed helping the Creole cook in their kitchen back home, even though her mother always said that cooking was for paid servants and not debutantes. Surveying the amount of food that still needed to be cooked on the counter behind Gladys, Sarah reached for an apron hanging next to the fridge and started chopping more mushrooms.

At the sound of chopping, Gladys turned around. "Oh no, dear, I didn't mean for you to help, I'm just complaining," she explained hastily. "Don't mind me; it's just Lila's been very unreliable over the past couple of weeks. I always manage to cope; I just don't know why I hired her, is all."

"It's no problem, I don't mind helping." Sarah's stomach growled in response and she added laughingly, "Especially if I can have some breakfast when we're done." She slid the mushrooms into a bowl and started slicing tomatoes.

Gladys laughed a throaty sound. "Of course you get breakfast, you are a guest! Which leads me to remember, we should still sign you in? I didn't even get your name last night?"

Sarah smiled and wiped her hands on her apron before holding them out towards Gladys. "Sarah Rothman."

Gladys took her hands in her wrinkled own and squeezed. "Welcome to Oak Cottages."

Sarah enjoyed the simple acquaintance; it wasn't like introducing herself in Savannah, where everyone knew who the

Rothmans' were, and immediately they set their own expectations of a Rothman on you. She was certain Gladys didn't even know about the Rothmans of Savannah. She started humming along with Gladys as they worked together on finishing breakfast.

After breakfast was served and all the guests left for the Convention in town, Sarah sat down to a leisurely meal on the front veranda overlooking the Mount Desert Narrows. The water seemed clearer here. The small waves were doing a slow dance with the shore. With centuries of practice, it slowly gained ground and gently receded. This was where she was meant to be.

Peace settled over her like a large warm blanket. She would stay in Blue Hill. Until it was time to go back.

She started making a mental list of things to do. Even if she planned to be away for quite a while, this wasn't a holiday. Without access to her credit cards, she needed to be realistic. The money left over from selling her car and buying the new 'old' car would be enough to accommodate the basic necessities for a few months, but she didn't have anything with her. Not even a toothbrush.

Hank gave her a fair price at such short notice but nothing close to the actual value of the Porsche. She'd need to go to town, get some clothes and basics. Then she had to find a job, not something flashy, something that paid by the hour, allowing her to still have free time.

During the long drive she had decided that she was going to start painting again. She'd need to budget in some paints; canvasses and an easel. She also didn't want a job that put her in the spotlight; so she could rule out the diner. In small towns everyone knew their favorite waitress.

She needed to speak to Gladys and find out what her rates were. Being a tourist accommodation spot, it was likely that if she stayed here, her money would run out in under a month, so she needed to find cheaper accommodation.

Her thoughts were interrupted when Gladys set a glass of orange juice down in front her, along with manila folder. "Fresh juice and your bill," she said with a smile. "The room you are in is open for a few nights yet if you'd like to stay longer." She sat down in the chair opposite Sarah and gave her a questioning look.

Sarah thanked her and opened the folder. The rates were more than reasonable compared to big city standards, but still nothing she could afford for more than a couple of weeks. "Could I maybe stay for a week, and then we'll take it from there?" she enquired as she signed the bill.

"Of course you can, dear. The convention people are leaving in the morning, so it will be just the two of us until next weekend." She sighed contently. "I always prefer having guests than staying alone in this big place." Gladys folded her hands in her lap as she gazed over the water. "I never get tired of this view."

"It's lovely; it has a certain peaceful melancholy about it." After sitting in companionable silence for a while enjoying the view, Sarah stood up, draining the glass of orange juice. "I'll just grab my purse and pay upfront for the week. I'll be heading into town, so I'll only be back later this afternoon."

Chapter 3

SARAH strolled through town taking in the lovely sights and sounds of Blue Hill. The small town fascinated her. People greeted each other on the sidewalk, waved to folk in vehicles. Everyone probably knew everyone.

She'd already managed to procure the clothing items needed for her stay. None of the designer suits and dresses she was used to. She had indulged on casual jeans and cotton shirts; her mother would have a slight heart attack. Next on her list was the drug store for toiletries. As she opened the door, a little bell chime went off.

"Be right with you," a muffled voice came from an open doorway in the back.

She grabbed a basket by the door, and browsed through the aisles, placing items she needed in the basket. Once she had retrieved everything on her list, she moved towards the cashier, a lady in her early thirties with a toddler on her hip.

"Hi there," she said in way of greeting as Sarah unloaded her basket. "Haven't seen you in here before?" She asked it unapologetically, with small town curiosity. Ringing the items up, she tried to keep the toddler from grabbing them out of her hands. She looked at Sarah and probed again. "Are you one of the convention people?" The toddler grabbed a bottle of shampoo and started chewing on the top.

"No, I just came into town last night." Sarah couldn't help but smile at the toddler who believed all his teething woes would be cured by chewing on the bottle cap.

"Oh dear." The lady realized what was happening and tried to pry the bottle from his hands. "Let me get you another one, this one is covered with drool."

"That won't be necessary," Sarah laughed and gently pulled the bottle from the toddler's hands while making funny faces. He gave a little laugh and his mother stopped his hands just in time from grabbing another item.

After Sarah paid, a thought sprung to her mind. "Is there perhaps an art store in town?"

"Oh yes, we have a little one down the way of the harbor, quite a few artists come round these parts to paint. Are you an artist?"

"No, I just like to play around a bit. Thank you and goodbye."

Leaving the store Sarah couldn't help but wonder why she felt a twinge of disappointment at saying she wasn't an artist. All her life that was exactly who she wanted to be, but her mother passed her love for painting off as a frivolous waste of time. She was to become nothing but the perfect wife, the perfect wife to Grant.

No else knew of her dream to paint. She knew she was quite good at it, with a sharp eye for texture and depth, and the combination made her paintings striking yet touching. She'd never had the time to hone her talent or the freedom to discover what she was capable of. As decided during the long drive, she would take the time in Blue Hill and explore her capabilities. This was something she felt she had to do. Not in secret as she did back home, sneaking away with her paints and easels. She would be able to do it freely.

Finding the art store quite easily, she managed to get all the supplies she needed to start out. She got a fright when it came to the bill; she had always just swiped her credit card with her allowance on, and this was the first time she had to work sparingly with her money. After the clothing, paying Gladys and the art supplies, there wasn't a whole lot left. She'd need to find work soon.

Sarah got back to Oak Cottages late afternoon and went upstairs to store her purchases in her room. The sun was starting to set through the window and it gave the room a soft glow. The four poster bed with its beautiful quilted bedspread looked inviting. The room was painted a welcoming soft butter yellow.

It was a shame she couldn't afford to stay here longer.

After unpacking her new wardrobe and amenities she went in search of Gladys, finding her in the kitchen sitting at the large island table in the middle with her head resting on her arms. Sarah pulled out a chair, which made a soft scraping sound on the wooden floor, startling Gladys.

"I'm sorry; I didn't realize you were asleep," Sarah swiftly apologized.

"I wasn't, not really. I was just hoping to gather enough energy to start cooking dinner." She rubbed her eyes and stretched her arms. "I always wanted my own establishment, it's just some days it's a lot of work, and my body doesn't enjoy the physical parts such as cleaning as much as it used to."

"I take it Lila still hasn't shown up for work?" Sarah inquired.

"No, and I don't think she'll show up tomorrow either, because then we need to dress down the bedrooms in the house and the cottages, and replace all the linens." Gladys got up and opened the fridge door. She took out baby potatoes, asparagus and more vegetables.

A thought came to Sarah's mind. "How about I help you out until the convention guests have left?"

"But you are a guest yourself; surely I can't expect that of you," Gladys replied, flabbergasted.

"You're not expecting it, Gladys, I offered." Sarah gently touched Gladys's elbow in a show of support. "It's not like I have anything else to do, and I like helping in the kitchen."

Gladys looked past Sarah out the window and thought for a moment. "Alright, I'll accept your help, on one condition." She looked at Sarah with a beaming smile. "You get two nights' stay on the house."

Sarah laughed. "That's fine by me."

The two of them worked in companionable silence preparing dinner. Their actions synchronized as if they had cooked together before. Cooking became a dance of anticipating each other's movements. Sarah loved it, the simple camaraderie. She enjoyed being useful, knowing she was making a difference in someone's day, even if it was just helping to cook dinner. She wasn't looking forward to making beds, but then all jobs had their downsides.

Dinner was enjoyed by the guests and could be called a raging success. Sarah smiled as Gladys accepted the compliments graciously, and then made her way back to the kitchen. She stacked the dishes, wiped the counters and scraped off the few plates that had leftovers on them. She had just finished packing the dishwasher when Gladys surprised her with a glass of Port.

"You deserve this," she said as she handed the glass to Sarah.

"Thank you, Gladys. Dinner was wonderful." Sarah took a sip of fiery liquid that warmed her from the inside. "Where did you learn to cook like that?"

Gladys sat at the kitchen island and started following the rim of the glass with her finger.

"I was a big fan of Julia Child; I watched all her television shows, read all her cookbooks. I was determined to be the greatest female chef this country had ever seen." She sighed softly. "Then I met George."

"George?" Sarah enquired as she pulled up a chair. The kitchen was clean, and now she could relax with a glass of Port and a stranger's memories.

"My late husband. We fell in love almost immediately. Got married a few months later. His father was fighting in Vietnam, so he couldn't attend the wedding. A few months later, we received news of his death. He died a hero in Vietnam. George inherited quite some money as he was the only child." Gladys started fiddling with a wedding ring on a chain around her neck. "Well, as I fell in love, my dreams started to take new shape. George and I started dreaming of having a place where we could entertain all day and make a living. So when this property came on sale, we didn't hesitate. We renovated it some, built the extra cottages and believed this is where we would grow old together." A wistful look settled in Gladys's eyes as she told the story.

"Please do continue, it sounds like a wonderful love story." Sarah encouraged.

"Oh, it was, dear." Gladys wiped tear from her eye. "We thought if we could run Oak Cottages together it would be the perfect life. I would cook for the guests, he would show them the sights and we'd always be together. Then he got drafted …" Gladys reached into her pocket for a handkerchief with little flower prints on it.

"He never came home, did he?" Sarah gently probed.

At Gladys's nod Sarah felt such empathy for this woman. She was so strong, so independent, yet the loss of George, her true love, still haunted her almost forty years later. It was that kind of love that Sarah wanted, not an arranged marriage.

"I'm truly sorry."

At those words, Gladys quickly wiped away the tears and blew her nose. "Don't you be sorry. I had the love of one of the greatest men the world has ever seen, I'm living the dream we had for each other, and living that dream allows me to feel close to him even forty years after I lost him." She put her hand on Sarah's. "Don't ever be afraid to love, Sarah. I can tell you're running from something, and I haven't pried and I won't. I've been around long enough to know you'll tell me when you're ready." She touched Sarah's hand. "But until then, just remember true love isn't something you can run from, it follows you."

"I'm not running from love." That was the most Sarah was willing to tell her at this time, and at least it wasn't a lie.

"Then at least I don't have to worry about a desperate man banging on our door in the middle of the night." Gladys let out soft laugh at her own statement.

The following morning Sarah was up early helping Gladys prepare and serve breakfast. After the guests had all checked out, her morning was consumed with collecting and changing linens. It was hard but satisfying work.

Once she was content all the chores were done she headed to the small study to browse the internet for work in the area. She found a site that boasted all available positions in Blue Hill, but once she started browsing, she frowned at the few positions available. She was glad when Gladys entered the study with a lovely tea set and petit fours on a tray.

"Come, sit down," Gladys summoned. "I see you're looking for vacancies in the area?"

Sarah stood up from the computer after closing the browser and went to join Gladys. "Yes, I am. But I can't seem to find anything that isn't either at the diner, the lumberyard or on a boat." She let out a woeful sigh.

"Maybe I can help you with that." Gladys looked at Sarah over the rim of her cup. "But before I can make any suggestions, I need to know how long you are planning to stay in Blue Hill."

Sarah picked up one of the delicate petit fours; the burst of flavors in her mouth was amazing, tart and sweet at the same time.

"This is wonderful!" She picked up her tea. "To answer your question, I'm not entirely sure." Sarah thought about lying to Gladys, but she had been so kind, maybe it was time to tell her why she was here. "If I hadn't ended up in Blue Hill, I would've been married by now."

She explained the whole story, from the initial planning of the wedding where her father and mother sat her down and explained how crucial this marriage would be to their wealth and their position in the community; to the moment where she pulled up at

Oak Cottages. Gladys listened intently without interrupting until Sarah was finished.

"Well, dear, I'm sure your parents have your best interests at heart, however I cannot fathom how they think they can force you to marry someone you don't love." Gladys shook her head, contemplating her own statement, and continued, this time sounding slightly pissed off. "On second thought, they didn't have your best interest at heart, a marriage without love is a business agreement, and the world has enough of those."

Sarah couldn't help but laugh. She didn't know what she expected Gladys's response to be, but she was grateful for it.

"I agree, and I have no idea how long it will take them to get over the fact that I'm not getting married. I thought a few months would give them some time to think and to realize this isn't a good idea, and if they still think it is a good idea, they'll know I'm not willing to be part of it. But for that part I need to grow a backbone first." She toyed with the rim of the glass before continuing in softer tone. "As long as I can remember, I've been pushed and manipulated into doing what they expected of me."

Gladys nodded, her eyes roaming the room as if searching for the right words. "Right. Well, we're going into autumn, and Oak Cottages still have a few bookings ahead before we close up for winter. How about I offer you food and board, and you help me?"

Sarah couldn't believe it; she might be able to stay in the lap of luxury. "But what about Lila?"

"Lila's had enough chances as it is, and I'm sure she's only still helping out because her mother and I are good friends. And if she really wants to work at Oak Cottages, there is more than enough for both of you to do. It'll lighten my load, and I won't have to worry about Lila not showing up whenever we have guests."

"I'd like that. Would I need to move to another room?" Sarah asked.

"No, that won't be necessary, unless ..." Gladys pondered a moment. "We won't be booked full again until next summer. I've checked the bookings and we have one cottage open until spring. You're welcome to it. I know that's a long way off, but at least you'll have the option, and it's one less cottage for me to worry about come winter, and that way you'll even have some privacy."

Sarah was elated. She'd have her own cottage, Gladys would be cooking her delectable meals, and she'd be able to work and live at Oak Cottages.

She stood up and shook Gladys's hand. "Thank you so much, Gladys. I promise you won't be disappointed."

"Well, come on now." Gladys stood and motioned towards the door, indicating Sarah should precede her. "Let's go take a look at your cottage."

As they followed the footpath toward the cottages, Gladys kept on chattering.

"It won't be a lot of work, and you'll still have plenty of free time. I'll mostly need you at breakfast and to do housekeeping.

Some days will be quiet, some days will be havoc."

Sarah laughed as she stepped onto a wooden porch. The view was even more breathtaking than on the veranda of the main house. There were two chairs and a small table where she could enjoy morning coffee or an afternoon read.

When Gladys opened the door the scent of lavender polish mixed with the musty smell of wood drifted out. Sarah eagerly stepped inside. It wasn't large, but it wasn't small either. Her gaze first settled on a heavy bookcase that stood below the window overlooking the Mount Desert Narrows. Adjacent to the bookcase was a small writing desk with a pad of paper and a desk light.

It looked cozy and inviting. She walked towards a beautiful log bed boasting a quilted bedspread in hues of orange and red wine. The earthy scent from fireplace and the comforting color scheme made her feel at home instantly.

She stepped into the en suite bathroom, and although it was small, the colors complemented the wood of the cabin. She turned away and noticed against the far wall there was a fireplace with a log pile. A comfortable couch rested in front of the fireplace; it wasn't as beautiful as it was inviting. A flat screen television was mounted above the fireplace.

The cabin boasted none of the luxuries and amenities Sarah was used to, but oddly enough she felt home.

She turned to Gladys. "I'll take it!"

After settling in and collecting her things from the main house, Sarah felt the temperature dropping. Autumn was different in

Maine than it was in Savannah. In Savannah it felt like you could finally breathe when summer subsided and autumn blew in. In Maine it felt clean and the air tasted new. She sat on her porch until it was time for bed, dreaming of new beginnings.

The following morning Sarah made her way to the main house after clearing out the cottages of dirty linens and empty supplies. A car was parked out front and she made her way round the back to enter that way. As she approached she heard voices in the kitchen. Gladys was chattering about the convention guests, and a male voice laughed. Sarah peered through the door, without Gladys and her guest noticing her.

"Lisa's in love again, this time it's a musician from Long Island," the man said with a faint smile touching his lips.

"Well, at least she's not hiding from love like you are." Gladys slid a cup of coffee toward him as Sarah stepped in. "Oh, there you are, Sarah; our next guest has arrived." She took Sarah's hand and led her towards the man.

Sarah was confused. "I thought we didn't have guests until the weekend?"

"Honey, Caleb has been coming here for so long, he's more like family, and strangely enough he's never shown up without me having a place to put him. Sarah Rothman, meet Caleb Sullivan."

He was tall; even sitting, Sarah could see this wasn't a small man. He was built with the taut muscled limbs and grace of an athlete. Dark brown hair; Sarah guessed it would appear black when wet. His eyes were the same shade of green the sea took on before a storm and when he looked at her and smiled, her heart nearly stopped. There was something in his gaze that felt like he could see into her soul.

When their hands touched, it sent tingles up her arms. Sarah had never had a reaction to a man before; it was completely foreign to her. She quickly withdrew her hand and crossed her arms, as if that would stop her response to this handsome stranger.

"Pleased to meet you, Sarah," Caleb said as he curiously watched her. He had felt the connection too and was no less surprised by it. "Are you the new housekeeper?"

"Well, yes, I mean no." Sarah stumbled, unsure of her new position, and looked towards Gladys for clarification.

Gladys felt the tension in the air and knew something more than an autumn storm brewed. "Sarah is helping out for a couple of months; she's staying in one of the cottages." Gladys headed to the coffee machine and poured some for Sarah. She handed her the mug. "Have a seat, dear. Caleb was just telling me about his sister's new boyfriend."

"We'll see if he lasts long enough for her to call him her boyfriend." Caleb said affectionately. He turned to Sarah. "You see my sister has this addiction to falling in love. And every time she does, she believes it will last forever." He picked up a biscuit from the plate Gladys had placed in front of them. "Until it doesn't."

Sarah merely nodded, not knowing how to react on

information about his sister's love life, when they had barely met.

Caleb and Gladys chatted amiably about his family and Oak Cottages, and Sarah felt left out. She had never been comfortable discussing her private life with strangers, and yet she wanted to be part of this easy banter and caring. She deduced from the conversation that he had two brothers and a sister. He lived in Wilmington, but came here frequently enough for Gladys to serve him in the kitchen.

When the cups were empty and the biscuits eaten, Gladys started clearing. "Caleb, it's been wonderful catching up and I do hope you stay for a quite a while?" Tea time was over and Gladys was back to business.

"I was hoping you could squeeze me in for at least two months." He looked at Gladys expectantly. "Maybe through winter if you'll have me?"

"I see," said Gladys conspiratorially. "This isn't just a visit is it? You're starting a new book?"

"Caught," Caleb threw his hands in the air. "Knew I wouldn't be able to come here without you sniffing out the truth. Can you fit me in?"

"I'm sure I can make a plan for you in one of the cottages, and if we do happen to have an overlap of bookings, you can just move to the main house for a night or two. But I doubt that, tourist season is coming to an end."

"Great." Caleb seemed pleased and asked pleadingly, "Same cottage, one at the end?"

"Yes, that'll be fine. You missed the masses by one day. We were full until this morning. Your only neighbor will be Sarah, so you don't have to worry about toddlers and tantrums next door, like last time."

Sarah sat quietly listening. Caleb would be her neighbor for as long as she stayed at Oak Cottages, both of them in their own cottages, out at the point. So there was no getting away from him and the butterflies he caused. Gladys mentioned something about checking her reservations and left the two of them alone.

Somewhere a distant bell of recognition chimed in her memory at his name. "You're a writer? Are you C.B. Sullivan?"

"Guilty as charged," he answered with an easy smile.

"I've read some of your novels. Mostly crime, isn't it?" Sarah had read a few of his books. They weren't just fiction. His novels were based on crimes solved by the FBI. The writing was exceptional, but the crimes and perpetrators sometimes highly disturbing. She always made sure to follow up with a romantic comedy.

"That's right. Is that a southern accent? Texas?" He redirected the subject smoothly.

"Savannah." As soon as the word left her mouth she wondered if he'd ever heard of the Rothmans of Savannah.

"I've never been. Heard it's a great place, why'd you leave?"

Sarah looked at him like a deer caught in the head lights, and immediately he knew that was not information she was willing to share.

"Sorry. I shouldn't have asked, my parents always complain I'm too curious."

Sarah was caught off guard; she should've known people would ask, and she needed to prepare an answer for when they did. "Don't worry. I was travelling a bit, and when I reached Blue Hill I thought I'd stay awhile." That wasn't exactly a lie.

Caleb, being very intuitive about people, knew this wasn't the whole story, but he'd leave that for another day. "I'll get my bags from the car and head on up to the cottage."

"I'll fetch the keys from the office and meet you there," she answered; showing guests to their quarters was now part of her job description. Even if the guests made her legs feel like molten marshmallows.

Sarah met him out front with the cottage keys. Since he knew the way, she fell into step beside him. She couldn't place the dark writing of C.B. Sullivan with this sociable handsome man. Somehow she had always pictured a dark and disturbed writer, with nothing but his typewriter and gloomy room for company.

"You keep looking at me funny." Caleb stopped.

"Oh, I'm sorry, it's just I never imagined you like this." Sarah indicated to the expanse of Caleb.

"Well, thank you, Ma'am. I think that is a compliment." Caleb raised his one eyebrow in question.

Sarah laughed; his easy humor was a fresh change compared to the politically correct men she was used to meeting. "I wasn't talking about your appearance," and she pressed her lips together as in thought. "Only."

"You can't leave me hanging, explain."

"I thought you'd be a miserable old man hunched over a typewriter with gray hair and a cigarette dangling from your lips."

Caleb laughed a deep baritone sound. "Give it a couple of weeks." He started walking again. "Everything about your mental image is correct except for the typewriter, and the cigarettes." He patted the laptop bag he had over his shoulder. "Why do you think I come here to write?"

"The view?" Sarah asked as she looked towards the water.

"That, and the fact that no one can put up with me when I'm writing. The first year I nearly bit Gladys's head off twice for trying to change my linen. The second year she realized when I do surface for air is the only time she can descend and spring clean the cottage."

They reached the cottage and he set the bags down at the door, turned around to absorb the view that had always cured him of writer's block.

Sarah moved to go but tripped over the bag at her feet.

Caleb caught her by the arm in time to stop the fall. "Careful now, you won't be much help to Gladys with a broken leg." He meant it as a joke but mid-sentence his voice turned husky as his eyes connected with hers.

Sarah couldn't move. Both were aware of the frisson of excitement, which suddenly heated the air. His touch was warm and firm and she could feel the power in his arms; his eyes were hypnotizing, she could get lost in those eyes.

She swiftly pulled her arm free. "I'm fine." She turned and walked away.

"I'll see you at dinner," Caleb said to her retreating back, glad he had the same effect on her as she did on him.

If only he knew what affect that was. He'd experienced desire, small bouts of fascination, but he'd never felt like his wind was punched out after looking into a woman's eyes. Her eyes were beautiful, but he'd seen blue-eyed blondes before. He'd explore this feeling later; right now he needed to set up his work space.

Chapter 4

SARAH walked swiftly towards her cottage. She didn't understand why, but she felt she knew him, and yet she knew nothing about him. When he touched her arm, she hoped he would touch more.

When he looked into her eyes she felt he could see her soul. She had not been allowed to date before going to college and since she returned from college, she was constantly seeing Grant. They had an easy friendship. There were no sparks or flutters involved. They both knew what was expected of them, and obliged by becoming friends. They had explored being lovers once after too much wine. The whole encounter was uncomfortable, to say the least, and a painful one for Sarah as well. They had mutually decided to figure out the sex after the wedding. They kissed on occasion, but that was always brief and sweet. Sarah had a feeling that when Caleb Sullivan kissed someone there would be nothing sweet and brief about it. After that horrible encounter, Sarah had never wanted to have sex again. Now heat pooled to her groin after one encounter with Caleb that wasn't sexual in the least.

She collected an easel, a clean canvas and some art supplies, deciding to empty her mind on a clean canvas. Painting had always soothed her whenever she felt that she didn't have control or felt manipulated.

Her parents forced her to attend college after school, while Grant attended Savannah State to become a lawyer. As a career was out of the question for their debutante daughter, and finishing schools no longer existed, they gave Sarah a choice of school. She chose Savannah College of Art and Design. Her mother saw it as a way to pass the time and hopefully learn something about interior decorating, but Sarah had decided to pursue art and enjoyed every minute of it.

One of her art teachers wanted to show Sarah's work in a gallery and her parents refused, believing it would encourage the spark that would lead her to pursuing a career in art.

When she returned from school, her mother explicitly told her that no artsy-fartsy ways would be accepted, and she wasn't to see an easel or smell paint around the house. So Sarah had painted in secret ever since.

Walking out of the cottage with her easel and supplies felt wonderful. She could go and sit to paint the Mount Desert Narrows without justifying the need to anyone. She set up her easel and started with slow brush strokes and definitive lines, and completely lost track of time.

Caleb found her there hours later on his way to dinner. She sat at the edge of the water, the soft rays of the sun creating a golden glow shining through her hair. She was completely consumed with the task at hand. He moved closer to see what she was working on. The watercolor was striking, the blended colors creating a likeness to the image of sunset over Mount Desert Narrows.

"That's quite a talent you have there," Caleb observed out loud.

At the sound of his voice Sarah startled and dropped a brush. "I didn't even hear you coming."

"On my way to dinner." Caleb moved toward the easel and studied the painting with interest before turning to her, their faces mere inches apart. "Would you like me to wait for you?"

Sarah could feel the heat of his breath on her skin, suddenly aware how cold it had become with the sun setting behind Blue Hill Mountain.

She couldn't force herself to pull away from the intimate way he was looking at her, but knew if he followed her up to her cabin now, she might feel the need to explore the finer details of love making with him.

"No, you go on ahead; I'll be there in a few." She stood up and turned away from him to gather her supplies.

"Alright, see you later," Caleb said and headed towards the main house.

Sarah briskly walked to her cottage and stowed her supplies. On her way to the door she caught her reflection in a mirror. It startled her for a minute. Her hair that was always perfectly styled was wind-blown. Her cheeks had a rosy tinge and her eyes appeared bluer than ever. She couldn't go to dinner like this.

She looked refreshed, if a bit wild. Even if her mother wasn't there to criticize, she should at least put on a fresh shirt and grab a cardigan. Not having much of a wardrobe to choose from, she selected a plain white t-shirt and a dark blue cardigan and quickly pulled a brush through her hair. It wasn't perfect, but Sarah didn't feel the pressure or the inclination to look perfect in Blue Hill.

As she entered through the kitchen, which had by now become a habit, she was met with jovial scene. Gladys was removing a serving dish from the oven, which Sarah suspected to be lasagna, Caleb sipped on a glass of red wine, and a beautiful young brunette was laughing at something he said. Feeling a bit out of place, ingrained manners pushed Sarah forward to introduce herself.

"Hi, I'm Sarah Rothman." She extended a hand in greeting.

The brunette jumped up and swiftly hugged Sarah. "That you are and also my saving grace." She let out a giggle and took both of Sarah's hands in hers. "I'm Lila Swanson."

Sarah was completely baffled. This was the girl who had let Gladys down a number of times, whose job Sarah was doing, and now she called Sarah her saving grace.

At her confused expression, Lila pulled out a chair and indicated for Sarah to sit. "I came earlier this evening to talk to talk to Gladys. She probably told you how unreliable I've been."

Sarah nodded, not sure if she followed. She looked to Gladys, hoping she could bring some light to the situation.

Gladys smiled at her. "Relax, honey, no one is throwing you out; give the girl a chance to explain."

Lila giggled again, and Sarah took in her image. She seemed very young. Sarah was only twenty four, but Lila had a naivety about her.

"You see, me and my boyfriend Mitch has been together for two years and a couple of weeks ago I realized I was pregnant." She raised her eyebrows at Sarah in an expression that said the pregnancy wasn't planned. "So it's been a rough couple weeks, deciding what to do, and I didn't want to come to work before I'd seen the doctor, I was afraid I could hurt the baby."

She took a sip of water and steamrolled on. "The doc says the baby is fine, and I can still work, just no heavy lifting and straining activities. So Mitch suggested I work for him at his auto repair shop. His receptionist resigned ages ago and he hasn't found someone new yet. But I didn't want to agree to that before I had a chance to speak to Gladys. Then Gladys told me about you!"

She jumped up and gave Sarah another hug.

Caleb noticed that Sarah wasn't very comfortable with Lila's easy displays of affection, but merely sipped his wine, reveling in watching Sarah trying not to look uneasy.

"I'm really glad I could be of help," Sarah said uncertainly.

"You should be as glad as I am," Lila insisted. "Oak Cottages is a wonderful place to work, and Gladys is like a second mother to me. I'm sure she's already taken you under her wing as well."

Sarah glanced at Gladys and smiled; finally Lila said something she could agree with. "She is lovely." Sarah accepted the glass of wine Caleb offered her, ignoring the frisson of excitement at his touch. "Seems like you have a lot going on at the moment, all good. I'm happy for you."

Lila nearly squealed. "You haven't heard the best part, Mitch asked me to marry him today!" Lila beamed. "So in a few months I'll be his wife, we'll work together and have a new baby."

"Rather you than me, Lila, but congratulations," Caleb offered with a sour expression.

"Oh, Caleb, don't be such a worry wart. Not everyone is as pessimistic as you are," Gladys admonished him. "Lila dear, I'm very happy for you. I'm sure your mother already started crocheting baby booties."

"You know her too well, she started yesterday. Yellow pair, as we want to keep the baby's sex a surprise," Lila answered.

"Will you stay for dinner?" Gladys asked as she started taking out plates.

"No, thank you, I must be off, my fiancée is waiting for me." She floated from person to person, accepting congratulations and bidding them a good night before she left.

"Right," Gladys said with a shake of head, "I've had about as much excitement as I can take in one day. Shall we eat?"

Sarah and Caleb agreed. Sarah picked up the tableware to take to the dining room.

"Don't worry about eating in there," Caleb stopped her. "Gladys and I normally eat in the kitchen when there are no other guests."

"That's right, Sarah. You can just set them out on the island counter, we can eat here." Gladys confirmed. "But first sit down and enjoy your glass of wine. Lasagna likes to be left to rest a little."

Dinner was a comfortable meal between friends. Sarah enjoyed two more glasses of wine. She never had more than two glasses on any occasion in her life. She could understand why most people did. She felt relaxed, footloose and fancy free. She listened to the conversation between Gladys and Caleb. They were more friends than host and guest. They chatted about the weather, Caleb's previous visits to Blue Hill and about Caleb's family.

After the dishes were cleared and stacked in the dishwasher it was time to retire. She bid Gladys a good night and started for the cottage.

A few steps into the twilight she heard Caleb coming up behind her. "Wait up."

Sarah stopped and turned; his long legs swallowed the distance between them with a few strides. "Afraid of the dark, C.B. Sullivan?"

"Not at all; afraid some fans might lurk behind the bushes and do unthinkable and pleasurable things with me."

Sarah laughed.

Caleb liked her this way. She was more approachable when she was a little tipsy. "Oh wait, you are a fan …" his voice trailed off in thought.

Understanding dawned in Sarah's eyes. She was playing with fire but couldn't help but flirt back. "Yes, I am." She looked him squarely in the eye, and stopped. Caleb followed suit, watching her expectantly. "But don't worry, Caleb; you're in no danger from me at all." She smiled and started walking again.

"Oh yes, I think I am," Caleb muttered to himself as he started after her.

As they reached Sarah's cottage, Caleb decided against walking her to the door, but it was like an invisible pull was forcing him to follow her up the steps.

"I'm not inviting you in, Caleb," Sarah said on a smile as she opened the door.

"I wasn't expecting you to."

Sarah turned to bid him good night, but hadn't realized how close behind her he was standing. She stood close to his chest; she could smell the fresh sea air and faint traces of after shave from his shower that morning.

She looked up at the same time Caleb looked down.

"Goodnight, Sarah."

She watched as his lips formed her name and couldn't help but think what they would taste like. Following instinct as old as mankind, Caleb slowly closed the distance between their mouths.

"This isn't a good idea," Sarah whispered against his lips.

Caleb felt her breath on his lips. "I've never had a better one." With that he bent and touched his lips to hers.

It was a slow soft kiss. He barely brushed her lips and kept them against hers for what felt like forever to Sarah. She savored the feeling of his lips; she felt his hand reach behind her back, to mold her to him.

His arousal through the jeans he wore pressed against her belly. She wanted; she wasn't exactly sure what, just more. She reached behind his head and tangled her fingers in the hair at his nape and pulled him even closer. Caleb teased the seam of her mouth open with his tongue. He could taste the red wine on her breath, with her essence mixed in.

Sarah opened her mouth with abandon. Their tongues started a slow dance. If a tsunami reached the shore, they wouldn't have noticed. They were caught up in exploring the new taste, and feel of each other, savoring each second.

Finally Sarah pulled away. "That shouldn't have happened." She touched her lips with her fingers, finding them wet from their kiss.

Caleb looked into her eyes; they were a stormy blue from the passion that consumed their kiss. "I'll agree it probably wasn't a good idea, but there's no turning back now."

Before Sarah could respond he had taken her mouth again with a hunger she had never experienced before. There was nothing soft and slow about this kiss. Sarah had no doubt about the desire Caleb felt as he pressed his body against hers.

He felt her reticence and coaxed a reaction from her; Sarah reveled in the feeling of his body against hers. For the first time in her life she experienced desire. It was a heat burning low in her belly urging her not to stop. It was *that* heat that forced her to stop.

She couldn't let this happen. She knew his reputation. He didn't commit. He had a new set of elbow candy at every press event, and Sarah had enough to deal with without being his holiday entertainment. She pried herself away and coolness settled in her eyes.

"I don't know what just happened, but I can assure you it won't happen again." She walked into the cottage and firmly shut the door behind her.

Caleb shook his head and a smile tugged at the corners of his mouth. "And I can assure you, I'll make sure it does," he said as he followed the steps down.

Chapter 5

THE following two weeks were a blur of activity around Oak Cottages. Guests arrived constantly, and by the end of the second week Oak Cottages was fully booked. It was time for the town's annual fair. The Blue Hill Fair attracted visitors every year from all around Maine and even out of state.

The small town was bursting at the seams with families, vendors and spectators. For Sarah it meant working harder than she ever had before in her life. She loved every minute of it.

From dawn to dusk she was busy with changing linens, cleaning up rooms, welcoming guests, serving breakfast and making supply runs to town. Never before had anyone relied on her as Gladys did or trusted her enough to give her large tasks.

It gave her a sense of being needed, and a sense of achievement as well, to know how much Gladys appreciated and came to trust her in the short time she'd been at Oak Cottages.

The days were too busy to give the thoughts of Caleb a chance to intrude into her mind, but at night when all was quiet, she would think back to that kiss.

That first night meeting him was like a dream; she frequently thought she might've imagined it. He'd been scarce since that night, but Gladys paid no mind to it, saying that when he went into his hibernation-mode; he was to be left alone.

"He'll come up for air when he needs it," she assured her when Sarah expressed worry over the fact that he hadn't been to the main house in two days for meals.

When he did come, he ate breakfast in the kitchen barely saying two words to Gladys. Sarah didn't have a chance to ask how the book was going, since she was serving in the dining room.

The last morning of the fair, after all the guests had left for the day, Gladys cornered Sarah in the kitchen with a mischievous look in her eye. "Go on, grab a coat and your purse; we're going to the fair."

"What? Now?" Sarah asked. "But we have so much to do still. We need to sweep the porches, I need to dust the living room, and I haven't vacuumed the guest rooms and cottages yet."

Gladys picked up her purse and draped a scarf round her neck. "That can wait. And tomorrow almost all the guests are leaving, then we can do a good clean." She took Sarah by the arm and moved her to the back door. "Go on now, you haven't been to the fair, and it's a shame to live in Blue Hill and not attend the fair. I'll give you five minutes to meet me by the car."

With that she closed the door.

Sarah shook her head as she headed toward her cottage. Gladys was a dear woman and as Lila predicted in the short time she'd been there, Gladys had become like a second mother to her. She loved her mischievous streak, even if Sarah felt as if she was playing hooky by not finishing her work.

A few nights ago a businessman, staying for one night, commented that the carpet in the foyer must've come from the same era as his grandmother and Frank Sinatra, not in a good way.

Not letting the comment pass, Gladys made sure that evening during dinner Frank Sinatra was on replay the entire time, instead of the community radio station that normally played.

Laughing to herself, she noticed Caleb walking towards her. He was wearing a scowl and muttering to himself.

"Careful, if the clock strikes, that scowl might stay there." Sarah teased.

"I don't have time for your childishness now," he muttered and briskly moved passed her.

Sarah was completely shocked by his comment and turned to stare at him. She couldn't believe this miserable unhappy person was the same Caleb that laughed and flirted with her two weeks ago.

Instead of feeling anger towards his comment, she felt sorry for him. It had to be lonely in that cabin with nothing but crime and horror surrounding him.

Maybe true talent did suffer to create greatness.

She quickly gathered her things and went to meet Gladys at the car. "Did you see Caleb?" Sarah asked as she closed the door of the hatchback Gladys drove.

"No, why?"

"He passed me on the way to the cottage, wearing a scowl. He looked really unhappy."

"He probably went to get his supply basket from the kitchen. I told him we might be going out and packed him a few snacks and sandwiches for today." Gladys started the car and headed down the driveway into town. "The first time Caleb came here, before I knew he was a writer, I was convinced he was doing more in that cabin than just having scotch and time to himself. I had to stop myself from calling the police to search for drugs. It kept on like that for close to six weeks."

Gladys continued as she easily maneuvered the hatchback through the traffic in town. "Until one day he came in for breakfast, shaved clean and wearing a relieved look." Gladys swiftly parked and turned toward Sarah to finish her story. "He told me 'now the worst part is over, he can put the demon away'." She gave a soft laugh. "I thought he meant he beat a drug addiction. It was only later he explained to me that when he is writing for a while he feels like he is the monster in the book he is writing."

"Oh, that's sounds horrible." Concern touched Sarah's eyes.

"It must be. From then on I leave him be, until he is ready to be himself again. I suggest you do the same."

Gladys opened her door and stepped out indicating the conversation was over.

The sounds and smells of the fair embraced Sarah. Children laughing, fair music and excited screams of the kids on the rollercoaster. The fresh salt breeze drifting in from the sea carried with it hints of popcorn, candy floss and roasted nuts.

They walked for hours perusing everything from paintings and pottery to homemade cheese and second-hand books.

Gladys excused herself to visit with a friend who had a home-made jam stall. "You go on, dear, I'm going to let my legs rest and do some chin wagging."

Sarah wandered through the rest of the stalls and treated herself to candy floss. She bit into the sugary sweetness and discovered she liked it. She felt like child again, without the strict adult supervision that tainted her childhood. She had such a regimented life back in Savannah. She was never good enough; her hair perfect enough or her manners perfected enough.

The past few weeks in Blue Hill had revealed more about herself than Sarah had ever known.

Without the expectations and criticizing eye of her mother watching over her, she was enjoying getting to know the real herself.

She learned that she loved the way the candy floss dissolved on her tongue and left a sweet strawberry taste.

She despised tailored pants. She had before only been allowed to wear jeans at home when no company was expected. Now she lived in them. They were comfortable, durable, and Sarah liked the way it shaped her behind.

Back in Savannah she was always the perfect debutante daughter her mother wanted, until the night her perfect little word had come tumbling down.

Sarah allowed herself, for the first time since arriving in Blue Hill, to think back on the events that had caused her to run from her own wedding.

It was a dinner party her mother had hosted, one of the many she hosted every summer.

That night Sarah was in the wrong place at the wrong time. She didn't mean to eavesdrop, but when she heard her father's name brought up between two young women, she couldn't help but listen in …

"So is Daniel Rothman finally going to divorce that wife of his?" a redhead asked the beautiful young brunette at her side. Sarah guessed her to be no more than a few years older than herself.

"I don't know. I don't expect him to. He takes good care of me," the brunette let out a sexy laugh, "and I take good care of him."

"But it's been almost five years; don't you want him to yourself?"

"Of course I do, but his daughter is planning her wedding and it isn't the right time now to ask him. Maybe after his daughter is married."

"I hope so; you can't go on being a scarlet woman forever."

Sarah was so shocked she went upstairs, retiring for the night without even excusing herself.

The next day she found her mother alone on the patio. She hinted at her mother using her impending marriage as an excuse.

"Mother, how do I know that Grant will remain faithful?" she cautiously asked.

"You don't, dear," her mother answered bluntly. "Men weren't made to be faithful, and if he does happen to stray, you don't ever mention it." Her mother continued watering her orchids, as if they were talking about the weather.

Her nonchalance caused Sarah to ask more directly. "Mother, has father ever strayed?"

At that question her mother turned around. "Sit down, Sarah."

Sarah obliged and joined her mother at the small wrought iron table placed on the patio.

"Do you like the way we live, the cars, the clothes, and the money?" her mother asked her seriously.

"Yes, of course, but …" Before she could finish her sentence her mother cut her off.

"There are no 'buts', Sarah. Your father takes good care of us, we have never wanted for anything. So if he goes to some brunette to satisfy his primal urges, I won't stop him. And I won't mention it. My job as his wife is to keep him happy and if that includes interludes with her, I'm not going to object and ruin the good life and name we have."

"You can't possibly mean that," Sarah said incredulously.

"Yes I do, and when Grant does stray - they all do, dear - you'll do the same. Rothmans don't air dirty laundry in public." Her mother stood, indicating that the conversation and lesson was over.

Sarah was shocked. Her father had an affair and her mother kept quiet for the sake of money and status.

The conversation with her mother haunted her up until her wedding day.

The morning of her wedding she was busy fixing her veil and looked out the window to where the guests were gathering. A movement caught her eye. She saw her father walking with the brunette towards the back of the house.

Sarah knew then she could not give up her life and dreams only to become like her mother. She didn't know if Grant would one day cheat on her. The society they were a part of obviously had no scruples about it.

All her life choices had been made for her.

All that was expected of women was to always look and act the way it was expected of them, and behind closed doors men had mistresses without their wives even batting an eyelid.

It was then she decided to run.

That was at the heart of escaping her wedding. What if she couldn't satisfy Grant? Their friendship would be ruined and she'd be living a life Grant wanted, not she. Their first and only attempt at sex had been horrible, and she wasn't sure it would improve after the wedding. She wouldn't have her own career to fall back on; she would be beholden to him.

That was why she needed the time in Blue Hill.

She needed to discover Sarah, and maybe when she did she could find out if she was good enough. Good enough to be happy with herself. That was why she didn't want to pursue the attraction she felt for Caleb. He didn't even hide the fact that he had many lovers and didn't commit. She couldn't bear being tossed aside for the next best thing. Sarah wouldn't allow herself to get close enough to man for him to be able to hurt her like her father.

Her mother had to be right, all men strayed. There were probably a few that didn't, but she didn't want to take a chance and fall in love with one that did. Maybe her mother didn't train her well enough, but Sarah knew she wouldn't be able to keep quiet and look the other way.

Caleb entered the kitchen, and opened the pantry door. There was a basket on the floor with a note on:

Snacks to help chase the demons away.

He smiled at Gladys's intuition, grabbed the basket and headed back towards his cottage. He was making progress with the book; the villain was escalating with the level of brutality in which he killed his victims.

When he was consumed with his writing like he was at the moment that was his only focus. He didn't allow ordinary routines such as eating and shaving to interrupt him. If he felt like a shower, he took one, if he was hungry, he would grab something from the snack box he stocked in the corner.

He forced himself to go to breakfast at the main house at least every second day, and ordered in pizza a few times. When he wrote his first book, he promised himself he would never put himself through that torture again, but then there was another story he needed to tell, and after that another. If he didn't write them the words would haunt him until he put them down on paper.

He felt bad for snapping at Sarah earlier, but it was better she saw this side of him. It kept woman from wanting to stay. If they stayed, he would hurt them.

And if he didn't hurt them, he lost them, like Elizabeth. As it often did, his thoughts drifted to ten years ago, when he was young and in love. They'd been high school sweethearts, engaged to be married. A month before their wedding day Elizabeth had worked late and on her way home a drunk driver ran a red light right into the side of her car. She was dead by the time the ambulances arrived.

The pain and guilt was still as fresh now as if it happened yesterday.

His family and her family all told him it wasn't his fault. But he couldn't help but think if he'd gone to get her that evening like she asked, instead of her driving home tired, late at night, the accident could have been prevented.

They had a fight before she left for work that morning; he wasn't paying enough attention to the details of the wedding.

She died doubting his love for her. He couldn't get himself to fall in love with someone again as he did with Elizabeth. Maybe she was his true love, if such a concept existed.

Ever since Elizabeth passed, Caleb only had affairs, quick, unemotional, uncomplicated affairs. He ended things before attachments were formed. His heart was closed off. He knew he no longer had it in him to love someone with that intensity.

He could tell from meeting Sarah that she had her own demons to slay, and she wouldn't be the type of woman that would be satisfied with a brief uncomplicated affair. And yet, he couldn't stop thinking about the kiss they had shared. It had the intensity of a summer thunderstorm and the gentleness of soft rain.

Chasing those thoughts away, he grabbed a sandwich and let himself be pulled back into a horror story where a man raped and killed young girls and then discarded them as trash.

Chapter 6

THE fair guests had all checked out a few days after Labor Day weekend and it was back to just Gladys, Caleb and Sarah at Oak Cottages. Sarah was sitting on her porch painting the sunset when Gladys came rushing towards her.

"Sarah!" she called out as she came closer.

Seeing the fraught expression on Gladys' face, Sarah dropped her brush and ran towards her. "What's wrong, are you ill? Should I call a doctor?" Sarah searched Gladys's face for signs of illness.

"I'm fine, dear, it's not me. My sister just had a stroke. Thank the heavens it wasn't fatal, but I need to go to her."

"Of course, would you like me to take you?" Sarah asked.

"No, no it's not that. She lives in Pennsylvania." Gladys was out of breath from the exerting run to the cottage, combined with the shock.

Sarah took her hand. "Come sit down, you'll keel over if you don't." She led her towards the porch and sat her down in one of the chairs. "I'm going to fetch you some water."

Gladys nodded, short of breath.

When Sarah returned Gladys was breathing more steadily.

"Thank you, dear."

"It's no trouble. Now tell me what can I do?" Sarah asked, concern lacing her voice.

"Can you take care of Oak Cottages for me? I don't know how long I'll be away, but it won't be more than a few weeks, I'm sure."

"Of course, Gladys, after all you've done or I how can you even doubt that?"

"I don't doubt it; it's just a lot of work. We still have a couple of weekend bookings for the next month until we close for winter. So you'll have to do everything yourself."

"Gladys, I'll manage," Sarah answered confidently. It was the first time anyone had expected her to do something of value and trusted her to do it. She was eager to prove to Gladys that she could.

"I can call cancel the bookings, yes, maybe I should do that." Gladys said as if the thought only occurred to her.

"You'll do no such thing," Sarah answered firmly. "You're going to go pack your bags and I'll drive you to the airport."

A tear slipped over Gladys' soft cheek. "The good Lord knew when he needed to send you to me."

With that she gave Sarah a brief hug and headed off to the main house to pack.

Sarah quickly stored her supplies and headed up to help Gladys and take her to the airport.

It was late evening when Sarah got back. She stopped on her way back from the airport and picked up a couple of pizzas. She knew she didn't have to cater for Caleb in the evenings, but they left late afternoon without even making sure he had helped himself to lunch.

She locked her car and walked toward their cottages. She contemplated at first pouring herself a glass of wine and enjoying the pizza before taking him his. On second thought, she needed all her faculties working around Caleb, and she'd rather just get it over with.

Stepping onto his porch, she knocked before thinking better of it. She heard a few muffled curses coming from inside. A few seconds passed before he opened the door.

He looked like a caveman. Unshaven, his hair messy from running his hands through it, and he wasn't wearing a shirt. The sight of his bare chest made Sarah momentarily forget why she was there.

"You better have a good reason for disturbing me," Caleb all but barked at her.

Sarah was quickly pulled from her reverie. "I bought you supper," she responded in the same tone. She shoved the box in his hand and turned to leave.

"I didn't ask for pizza!" he shouted after her. "Gladys knows not to interrupt me."

That was it. She'd had it. She had a lousy day, Gladys was counting on her to take care of Oak Cottages all by herself and her only guest was a raging buffoon.

She turned on her heel and strode toward him until she could look him straight in the eye. "No, you didn't, so the right thing to do would be to say thank you." He started to talk but Sarah held up her hand in a way that a mother would to keep a small child from talking. "I was out all afternoon and most of the evening, and didn't know if you'd been to the kitchen or not. I didn't feel like cooking if you were hungry, so I got pizza to make sure you had food."

Caleb looked at her like she was an alien from another planet. She made him feel foolish for snapping at her. "Where is Gladys, she knows how I work," he asked in an accusatory tone.

"Gladys has gone to take care of her sister in Pennsylvania, so you're stuck with me." Sarah all but shouted at him.

As soon as the words left her mouth, she knew it was inappropriate to speak to a guest that way. She took a deep breath and let the debutante in her takeover.

"Maybe we could arrange a time that would suit you, to come to an agreement of meals and housekeeping," she said in a cool manner. "Would tomorrow morning work for you?"

Caleb was fascinated.

She could go from hot to cold in a Matter of seconds. He wanted to watch her go hot when he was brushing his mouth along her curves. The one minute she was reprimanding him as if he were a child and the next she was the perfect southern belle.

"Caleb?" Sarah's voice cut through his thoughts.

"Yes, tomorrow morning will be fine," he replied, still disconcerted.

"Will you be happy with an omelet for breakfast?" Sarah asked. She didn't want tomorrow morning starting out on the same note.

"That will be fine," he answered in an even tone.

Sarah was already a few strides away when she heard Caleb call her name, and she turned around to see him still standing in the same spot holding the pizza box.

"Thank you for the pizza."

Before she could reply he had gone inside and shut the door. It was going to be a long two weeks with Gladys gone.

The next morning Sarah woke early. After a quick shower she made her way to the main house. She remembered an old homemade bread recipe from their cook back home, and after making sure the dough was knead enough, she headed upstairs to swiftly vacuum and dust all the rooms, including Gladys's. When she could smell the bread dough she headed downstairs and placed it in the preheated oven.

A quick look at the clock told her it was almost eight o'clock. She started getting everything ready for the omelets, when a sound at the door alerted her to Caleb's arrival and made her turn around.

He was clean-shaven, but the darkness of his mood was reflected in his dark green eyes.

"Good morning," came her forced chirpy reply.

This side of him attracted her. He looked real, like a man who knew pain, and who experienced emotions deeply, but it was the raw male sexuality and the power it held over her that fascinated her. If it wasn't for his reputation Sarah would've enjoyed getting to know him better. But she wasn't going to take any chances with her heart.

Caleb moved towards the kitchen island and sat down. "Smells good in here?" he questioned.

"Bread's in the oven. Would you like some coffee while I whip up your omelet?"

"That would be great, thanks."

Sarah felt his eyes on her back; it felt like he was touching her as tingles moved over her body. Ignoring the sensation she offered him his coffee.

He drank it down and promptly set the cup down. "Your brew is better than the standard Oak Cottages brew; just don't tell Gladys I said that."

"Thank you, I believe coffee is one of the few things in life where stronger really is better." Sarah cracked three eggs into a jug and started whisking.

There was an awkward silence in the kitchen as Sarah prepared the omelet with Caleb watching. Sensing Caleb was still in what he called his dark place; Sarah didn't attempt to make conversation. After setting down his omelet in front of him, she grabbed some coffee for herself and sat down with him at the kitchen island.

"This is great, thanks," Caleb said between bites.

Sarah couldn't help but stare; he ate like a starved man. After four bites the omelet was almost devoured.

"Can I make you another one?" she offered with a hint of laughter in her voice.

"That would be great, thanks, if it's not too much trouble."

"No trouble."

After the second omelet and two slices of freshly baked bread were devoured, Sarah sat down again.

"So about the schedule, would you like to explain to me what works for you?"

Caleb wanted to tell her that any position and any hard surface along with any degree of undress would work for him at this stage, but refrained and answered solemnly, "No interruptions."

"I understand that, Caleb, but you need to eat, and I need to clean the cabin." Sarah let out a resigned sigh. "This isn't an ideal situation for either of us. I know you and Gladys had your routine, but since she's not here, can we work out something?"

"Fine," Caleb said, chewing his cheek in thought. "How about this? Breakfast every second morning, and on the days I don't have breakfast you can leave a basket in the pantry for lunch?" He looked at her questioningly, but before Sarah could answer, he added, "That will keep me out of your way, and you from bothering me."

Sarah couldn't believe he could be so rude, but thought better than to call him on it. The look in his eyes this morning was different than the other times he teased her or scolded her. He looked raw.

"Fine."

Caleb was trying his best to be friendly, but the dark cloud still hung over him from the words he put on paper during the night.

Sarah's soft curves and friendly smile made him want for something he hadn't wanted in a long time - comfort. He was trying to convince himself it was only her proximity that attracted him. But in his heart he felt there was more to her. And he couldn't help himself, he wanted to know more. He wanted to touch her. But he couldn't. She wasn't the type of girl that he could roll around with tonight and look in the eye tomorrow.

The single kiss they shared haunted him. Made him ache from desire for one more taste, one more touch. But he couldn't. He had nothing to offer her but a roll in the sheets, and yet he felt he wanted to offer her more.

This was dangerous ground for a man who had avoided intimacy for the past ten years.

Sarah started clearing the dishes and loading the dishwasher.

He had never felt the need to apologize to anyone for his behavior when he was writing, but he needed to say something to her.

"Sarah."

He said her name with a scratchy voice, as if he hadn't spoken for years; he didn't mean to, he didn't know what to say to her.

Sarah turned around, and looked into those dark green eyes. They were completely focused on her. There air turned thick with desire, as their eyes met.

She didn't say anything. What could she say? 'I want to touch you, but I don't trust men?' Sarah knew she wouldn't be able to share her body with him without growing to feel something for him.

They looked at each other for what felt like hours.

Eventually Caleb got up and walked towards her. Taking her hands in his, he felt that rush again at the touch of her skin. "I'm sorry." The apology was simple; his voice rough.

Sarah's mind was completely blank. She tried to focus on the words, but the feel of his strong hands holding hers distracted her mind from any rational thought. What was he sorry for?

He started drawing small circles on her hand with his thumb. "I know I can be a bit of an ogre when I'm writing." He almost whispered to her.

Sarah just nodded; her body had never reacted this way when a man touched her. Grant's touch was always friendly, not electrical. She had temporarily lost the ability to speak. Her mouth was slightly open and she couldn't help but inhale his scent with a quick draw of breath. He smelled of citrus aftershave, and coffee, and the smell made her mouth go dry. How could her body and her heart betray her mind like this, she couldn't allow this to happen.

Caleb enjoyed the feel of her skin under his fingertips; her skin was soft and warm. She was looking at him with the same hunger he felt. He knew it wasn't the right thing to do, but he couldn't help himself. He bent down and touched his lips to hers.

She breathed a soft sigh into his mouth as he pulled away.

"It shouldn't be this way." Caleb thought, not realizing he said it out loud. "I'm going to hurt you," he added in a whisper to answer the confused expression on her face. Sarah was still looking at him, her eyes clouded with desire. "Don't look at me that way, or I won't be able to let you go."

Caleb didn't know if he meant the words for her or himself, either way he knew he was asking for trouble touching and kissing her.

Sarah put her hands in the tufts of dark hair at his nape. "I don't want to get involved with you." Her words meant one thing, but the way her fingers played at his neck said another. "I know your type …" She let the words trail off as she pulled her hands aside and tried to turn away.

He swiftly caught her arm and backed her into the counter. Their bodies were fused from the knees to the chest. "What type?" he asked in a dangerous tone. His eyes had gone from a troubled green to a dark and dangerous haze.

"You have a new girlfriend every week," Sarah said accusingly in barely more than a whisper. "You even take two ladies to one event." Her eyes had gone hard and she was looking at him reproachfully. Gathering all her courage she lifted her chin as she said, "I don't need that kind of man in my life, and I can promise you this …" She waved the air between them. "… this might be fun for you, but this isn't a game to me, Caleb. I don't want anything to happen between us."

Caleb looked furious as he swung away from her and pulled his hand through his hair. "My reputation? Really, that is your defense?" He picked up his jacket from the stool where he had set it down when he came in, and slipped it on. "Don't worry, I don't intend for anything to happen between us. I don't need a judgmental Southern Belle in my life." He opened the door and said to her before making his exit, "See you in two days."

"Two days too soon!" Sarah shouted after him.

How could such a confusing, rude man manage to heat her blood and make her mad at the same time?

Chapter 7

CALEB walked away from the house furious. He tried to stay away from her, he fought the attraction. He knew he would only hurt her, he couldn't bring himself to offer anyone more than one night.

But his type? He couldn't help what the magazines or publishers wrote about him. She was accusing him as if she had personal knowledge of his life.

This was the part about being a New York Best Selling Writer he hated. Everyone thought they knew him, and yet few really did.

He entered his cottage and headed straight for the laptop. It was time he learned a bit more about her. He typed her name into the search engine and a few clicks later he was reading about what Sarah ran from in the Savannah Tribune.

Sarah scrubbed the kitchen with bleach and brushed down to the paint. She couldn't believe Caleb admitted he was going to hurt her, and when she called him on it he got upset, no, not upset, furious. He was all but spitting venom from his eyes as he left the kitchen. She scrubbed until she failed to convince herself she wasn't attracted to him, and that she didn't enjoy the kiss.

If Caleb hadn't said anything, she would've offered herself to him right there on the cooker hood. She was mad at Caleb, but she was furious with herself. She shouldn't allow him to affect her this way.

Sarah drove into town later that afternoon to get supplies. As she passed a phone booth she thought she ought to at least let her parents know she was still alive. A phone booth would be a good idea to dial the home number from, for that way her parents wouldn't know where she was hiding out. She picked out a few quarters from her purse and called, and after a few rings the housekeeper answered.

"Rothman home, Gerty speaking," came the Creole accent.

"Hi, Gerty, it's Sarah. Are my parent's home?"

"Sarah, are you all right, child? You gave us an awful fright and left us with a mess, young lady."

The phone booth bleeped for more quarters. "Yes, Gerty, I'm fine, I don't have a lot of time, could you please call one of my parents to the phone?"

"Of course, dear, but only your father is home."

Sarah heard Gerty place the phone down and waited for her father to pick up.

"Sarah?" His voice came on, laced with concern.

"Hello, father," Sarah answered, the heavy weight of parental disappointment settling on her shoulders.

"Where are you?" He sounded exactly like the stern attorney he was.

"I'm not telling you," Sarah answered defiantly. "I'm safe, that's all you need to know right now."

"Sarah, stop this foolishness. Come home," came her father's terse reply. "I'm sure Grant will still have you if you explain to him you had a case of cold feet."

Sarah shook her head and made a sound of exasperation. "Don't you even want to know why I ran away?"

"That doesn't matter now, just come home so we can settle this."

"There is nothing to settle, I'm not marrying Grant or anyone else you have in mind and that's final."

"But Sarah …"

"No buts, father, I refuse to become like mother, turning a blind eye to the brunette you have in town. I refuse to be part of a society where a woman is treated like a possession."

"Sarah, what brunette?" came the nervous query from her father.

"Don't be coy, father, I know about her. I know about how mother just accepts it. Well, I won't, I don't love Grant, and I'm not getting married because you think it's a great idea."

"Sarah, it's not like that, you don't understand …"

Sarah cut him off; she hated hearing that guilty pleading tone from her father - he knew she knew. "I had my own great idea, and until you can accept me for who I am flaws and all, and stop trying to wed me off like it's the 18th Century, I won't be coming home. Goodbye, father."

She hung the phone up with a distinctive click. She had never spoken to either of her parents in that manner. Maybe it was time for things to be said, maybe then they would see her as an adult.

On her way back to Oak Cottages she switched on the radio to drown out the swirling thoughts about her parents.

The local station announced a storm moving in from the Atlantic; it was to hit land in about an hour. Sarah remembered Gladys explaining that sometimes bad weather could cut the power and the phones lines and to be prepared for such events.

On arrival, Sarah set about finding candles and setting out cold dinner for herself. She took the basket with supplies to her cottage when the first drops of rain started to fall.

As she approached the steps to her porch the first bolt of lightning struck with a loud *thwack*.

She couldn't stop the scream she let out before sprinting into her cottage and slamming the door behind her. She knew the lightning didn't strike close to her; she just wasn't prepared for it.

Laughing at herself and her skittishness, she set down her supplies and headed over to the fireplace to start a fire, when suddenly her door was ripped open and Caleb charged in, grabbing her by the arms

"Are you hurt?" he demanded furiously.

"No. Why?" she asked, confused.

"I heard a blood curdling scream and the door slamming," Caleb stated, still holding onto her. He assessed her for injuries or blood, anything to explain the scream.

Sarah started laughing, thinking of what it must've sounded like to the man in the cottage next door. "The scream was me, I got a fright when the lightning struck and dived head first into the cottage," she explained between bursts of laughter. "Good to know I have a blood curdling scream."

Caleb released her as the second roar of thunder shook the cabin windows and the lights started flickering.

Sarah walked toward the basket of supplies. "You should take some candles for if the power goes out." She barely finished her sentence when the cabin suddenly went dark.

Caleb looked at the basket suspiciously. "Do you have food in there?"

"I believe I do," Sarah said as she lit a candle.

"I lost track of time and didn't have a chance to run into town for supplies, mind if we share?"

"Sure," Sarah said as she stacked digestive biscuits, fruit, cheese, chocolate, preservatives and a variety of cold cuts on the table. "Grab what you need as well as some candles," she offered, indicating the spread on the small kitchenette.

The roar of raindrops on the roof became louder, indicating the heavens had just opened.

"Maybe you'd like to wait out the worst of it here?" Sarah asked politely, certain the answer would be no.

Caleb looked out the window, and although he'd never been afraid of getting wet, he wanted to stay. It wasn't a good idea, the desire he felt for her would most certainly gain the upper hand, but there was magnetic pull towards her he couldn't understand.

The power was out and he wasn't going to be able to work much longer than the battery permitted. He'd rather save the battery for later tonight and spend some time with Sarah.

A small voice in the back of his mind warned him against it, but this woman fascinated and confused him at the same time. And just maybe he could find out why Sarah Rothman of Savannah ran from her own wedding.

Trying not to sound too rude, he came across as sincere when answered Sarah with a glint of mischief in his eye, "That's sounds great thanks. It's not like I'd be able to work much with the power down."

Chapter 8

SARAH looked up; her eyes wide, her lips moist, shocked at his suggestion. He was arrogant, rude, and she had no desire to spend the evening with him. But excitement started heating her blood.

She was just being polite; this didn't mean something would happen, it didn't mean she wanted something to happen. This wasn't good. How on earth was she going to ignore him, when the two of them were stuck in a candle-lit cottage in the middle of storm?

Clearing her throat, she pushed a stray strand of hair behind her ear. "Right," she said and started opening packets and laying them on the single plate she had packed in the basket, "maybe you could add more logs to the fire?"

She needed him to move away from her so she could build her defenses against an evening with Caleb Sullivan.

Caleb obliged and placed more logs on the fire. He could see he was making her uncomfortable. He was glad to know the effect was mutual, but he also knew that when two small forest fires merged, the result could be a blaze of destruction.

He kept his distance and sat down in front of the glowing fireplace. Through his peripheral vision, he watched her.

She was made for candlelight. In daylight she was beautiful, with the sun catching her hair, her bright smile and her eyes blue as the Caribbean, highlighting all her features at once. In the candlelight, only some of her features were prominent, the soft glow of hair, her heavy eyelashes, her lips … Caleb felt his groin starting to respond and promptly began counting backward from two hundred as he moved to sit on the sofa.

Sarah joined Caleb on the only sofa, placed directly in front of the fire. Her only other option was the bed and she intended to stay as far away from that as long as Caleb was close. Heat was slowly seeping into the cottage slapping back the biting fingers of the cold.

She was at a loss for words.

Caleb wasn't in the jovial mood he was the night she met him, but he also wasn't the bear with a sore tooth. This was a different side of him. It seemed more real.

Both started picking off the plate and eating, intently watching the fire, ignoring all the things that were unsaid.

Caleb was first to break the silence. "Would you like some wine?" he asked. "I noticed there was a bottle in the basket."

"I completely forgot about that," Sarah's reply came quickly.

She didn't offer him wine, as the candlelight and fire was already a difficult atmosphere to fight. She hoped he didn't notice the wine.

"Let me get it," she offered, but Caleb pressed a hand on her knee. Both felt a jolt from that casual touch and their eyes met in the candlelight.

"No, let me," came Caleb's husky reply.

Sarah fought to repair her composure. The rain was thrashing against the window, and the wind was beating against the cottage. The storm just had started and was still building momentum. Sarah thought the weather was the perfect gauge for her response to Caleb.

"Here you go." Caleb offered her a cup.

She had forgotten to pack a wineglass, never mind two. They sat on the sofa, making sure they didn't touch, feasting on snacks and drinking wine from cups.

Caleb broke the silence after what seemed like forever. "I googled you," he said as he turned to face her.

Her eyes hardened before she answered him in a low voice, "You did what?"

"Well, you obviously know a lot about me, accusing me of being a certain type. I just wanted to find out your type."

"And did you?"

Caleb plucked a grape from the plate and popped it into his mouth, a teasing glint in his eye.

A slow smile spread across his face as he raised his eyebrows.

"Apparently the type of southern belle that runs from her own wedding."

Sarah went completely still.

"I hope the groom didn't take it too hard."

"That is none of your business," came her sneering reply.

"Don't be like that," Caleb said. "You apparently know everything about me from reading the papers, I just returned the favor."

"I think it would be better if you left now."

"But why, we're just getting to know each other."

"I have no intention of getting to know you better, none at all."

"Really?" Caleb mocked. "It doesn't seem that way when I touch you." He placed his arm on the back of the couch, his fingers barely grazing her neck. Sarah instantly stiffened. "Don't you want to know why that happens when we touch?"

"No, I don't," Sarah said, forcing herself not to react. She chastened her body for betraying her. If she moved to stand up now, she would only confirm that he did affect her, and she didn't want that either.

"So why did you run from your own wedding?" Caleb asked conversationally.

"I didn't love him."

"Then why get engaged?" Caleb asked, bemused.

Sarah didn't *want* to answer to Caleb, but maybe the atmosphere or the storm, or his fingers at the nape of her hair, caused her to answering resignedly, "My parents wanted us to."

Caleb picked up on the fatalistic tone, and couldn't help but delve deeper into the open wound Sarah was still nursing. "Sounds very 18th Century to me. Why did you go along with it?"

Was he going to stop asking questions? This wasn't fair, Sarah thought. If he wanted answers, she wanted a few of her own. "If you're not going to stop asking questions, you're going to be answering a few yourself."

She turned the tables on him, shifting in her seat, dislodging his hand in her hair, to look him straight in the eye.

"Why are you so miserable when you're writing?" she asked before he could object.

The answer he gave everyone including his family was easy - he didn't like interruptions - but he found himself telling Sarah the truth.

"It takes me to a dark place. A place where there are no happy ever afters, a place which exists in our world, but is shied away from, and hidden by society because they don't want to acknowledge what one person is capable of doing to another." Caleb spoke in a dark tone. "It's a place I'd rather not share, so I end up there by myself and I only manage to escape it once the story is written."

She didn't expect such an honest answer. Looking at him with concern in her eyes, she couldn't help but feel sorry for him. Not knowing how to respond to that, she responded to his question instead.

"My parents are prominent in Savannah Society. Since I was eleven, I was trained to be a debutante, how to walk, how to talk, how to dress. Decisions were always made for me. Any type of career was out of the question, a debutante's main goal in life is to support her husband according to my parents, and I was groomed to be exactly that." She gave a resigned sigh and continued in a sarcastic tone, "They told me on my eighteenth birthday that Grant, who had always been a good friend, was kind enough to accept me as his wife. The wedding would be a merger of two of the most influential families in Savannah. Being the obedient daughter that I was, I accepted it. I was allowed to attend an Art College while Grant was studying to be a lawyer; shortly after his graduation the engagement was announced."

She shrugged nonchalantly, indicating at the time she was resigned to her destiny as her parents had planned it.

"What changed your mind?" Caleb asked with the cup poised at his lips for another sip.

"Uh-huh, your turn first." Sarah gaze went to the ceiling as if the next question she wanted to ask was waiting for her there among the wooden beams, and she found it. "Why do you write crime novels?"

Caleb pursed his lips and almost started telling her the PR version his agent sold, when he decided against it.

This was the first woman he wanted to share something with since he lost his fiancée.

"When I was fifteen my friend's sister, Chloe, was kidnapped, she was tortured for ten days before being ruthlessly killed. Her body was found dumped in the river like trash. I was at an impressionable age, and I wanted to know why the guy did it."

He took another sip from the cup, savoring the dark liquid and absorbing the wooden flavors and smooth texture.

"I started reading about serial killers and what disorders or mental disturbances drove them to do the things they did. I decided I wanted to work in the Behavioral Analysis Unit at the FBI, consequently making that my life goal. Once I graduated high school I realized I wasn't the suit and tie type and I probably wouldn't allow the perps to get their day in court." He gave her a wry smile. "That dark side of mine comes with a filthy temper and an iron fist."

"And then how did you start writing?" Sarah prompted.

"When I turned twenty-one, the guy that kidnapped and tortured Chloe was caught. I went to court every day to support my friend's family. After the SOB was convicted and sentenced I found myself putting down on paper the psych evaluations that revealed exactly what drove him to do what he did and I couldn't help but tell Chloe's story in there as well. After about three months of very little sleep and writing between classes, I realized I had a book and, as they say, the rest is history."

"What did you study?" Sarah asked.

"Nope, you first. What was the final straw that turned you into a runaway bride?"

He had that mischievous look in his eye and Sarah couldn't help but smile at his phrasing before she answered.

What started out as an uncomfortable situation had turned into a soul-baring conversation? She had never felt comfortable revealing her feelings to people, but somehow she found herself wanting to confide in Caleb.

The lock of hair she was twirling around her finger at the side of her head was suddenly dropped and she folded her hands in her lap. "I found out my father was having an affair." Sarah said it in a bitter tone.

"Okay?" Caleb didn't understand at all how that connected with her wedding.

Sarah took a long sip of wine from the cup. "I hinted at my mother if she knew anything about it, and she came straight out and admitted knowing *all* about it." Sarah gave a wry laugh. "And then she proceeded to tell me if Grant cheated on me, which he eventually will, I was to turn a blind eye." She impersonated her mother's southern stern voice, "'Rothmans never air dirty laundry in public'."

Caleb frowned in disapproval. "Let me just get this straight. She actually overlooks it, and then tells you to do the same?"

Sarah ignored for a moment the fact that Caleb himself probably had cheated a few times, when he interrupted her thoughts.

"Maybe in Savannah, but in the real world cheating isn't overlooked, its frowned upon."

"Apparently that's how things work in Savannah society, the wives keep quiet and the men have their play of the field."

"So you ran from your wedding knowing it was going to be expected of you to be the faithful quiet wife at home?" Caleb asked for clarity.

"Exactly," Sarah smiled sadly. "Can you picture me in that role?"

"Nope, not at all," Caleb bantered. "You don't even take orders from paying guests."

Sarah laughed. "So that's my story." She shrugged. "Until my parents accept I won't be married off, I'm not going back, that is if I can ever look at my father again. How can I trust him after this?"

Caleb sighed. "That's not a question I have the answer to, but I can tell you he is still the same person, you only found a part of him you don't approve of." Seeing her raising her eyebrows at his statement, Caleb changed the subject. "More wine?"

Sarah nodded and Caleb stood to pour.

"So what did you study?" Sarah repeated her question of earlier.

"Journalism." Caleb offered her the cup of wine and sat down in front of the couch instead of on it. "But I never graduated. I only finished my second year, and then I had to do the book tour and never returned."

"So you wanted to become a writer?" Sarah asked as she took a piece of cheese from the plate.

"After I gave up on Quantico, I thought more along the lines of investigative journalism, not actual writing. It seems the profession chose me. Now there's always another story I need to tell."

"So what do you do when you're not writing?" Sarah asked.

"You're very sly, Sarah, you already asked two in a row, and it's my turn." He smiled at her teasingly.

Sarah had sat down on the couch with her feet folded underneath her and now shifted to pick up her wine cup; her ankle grazed his thigh.

Caleb reached down to her ankle and started to caress it through her jeans. "What did you want to do with your life before it was planned for you?" He spoke in a tone that sounded as if he was asking her for erotic favors.

Sarah's breath hitched, and she repeated the question in her mind before answering. "I wanted to paint."

His fingers were alternating between stroking and squeezing her ankle. When did that become an erogenous zone? Her mind fluttered back to his comment of earlier about her father's affair.

"How many times have you cheated?"

Caleb abruptly removed his hand from her ankle; he looked at her contemptuously, and then answered her question honestly.

"Not once." His brows pulled together disdainfully. "What gave you the impression that I did?" Sarah opened her mouth to speak, but Caleb held up his hand. "Wait, let me guess, the papers?"

"Caleb, I ..." Sarah wanted to apologize but he was already standing up.

"I think that's enough Q&A for tonight." He grabbed his jacket from the counter and starting putting it on.

"Caleb, I didn't mean to offend you, honestly."

Sarah stood up and walked towards him. She could see the hurt in his eyes when he answered her; she knew he was telling the truth. That still didn't mean she could trust him, but for this moment she was going to trust her heart.

"Don't go." She touched his arm. "Stay."

Chapter 9

CALEB watched as Sarah unconsciously ran her tongue over her lips to moisten them. She looked soft and inviting and he wanted nothing more than to spend the night. But would that be the right thing for both of them?

The desire he felt for her had already started to pool in his groin. He would like nothing more than to take her hard and fast and get her out of his system, but that wouldn't be right. He still mourned for his fiancée; she had lost her trust in men.

Tonight would be a brief interlude that would make the morning after uncomfortable. He knew she would regret it and he probably would too.

"Sarah, you and I both know where this is going to end up if I stay. I don't cheat, but I don't do relationships either, and you won't be able to cope with that." His voice was husky, barely more than a whisper.

Sarah felt the temperature in the cabin rise with desire and sexual tension. She had never experienced a man looking at her with raw craving in his eyes, and if there was one she couldn't at this moment even recall his name.

The only name she could think of was Caleb's. She understood exactly what he meant, that it would only happen once, no attachments, no explanations. She thought about how she would feel in the morning. Used? Beautiful? Wanton? Cheap? She imagined how she would feel about each of those words applied to her, and disregarded the thought completely.

In answer she kicked off her shoes and undid the band in her hair.

Caleb watched Sarah debate his warning. He could see her nipples already straining against the cotton shirt. He wanted nothing more than to tease them with his mouth. If she said yes, he would make sure this was one night she would never forget.

She would know what desire was.

A flame burning so fast and hard it nearly scalded your nerves from excitement.

He would offer her none of the polite friendly chaste kisses that arranged fiancée Grant had bestowed upon her. He would make sure she knew what it felt like to be wanted. As she let her hair fall, Caleb understood what she was saying with her actions. Accepting his terms, he heard her voice through the fog of desire clouding his mind.

"Stay."

Caleb fought away the voices that told him to leave; he had never wanted a woman so badly. Suddenly he was glad for the protection that Gladys had always provided in the bathroom cupboards; at least he didn't need to worry about that. He took her face in his hands and slowly caressed her cheeks before leaning toward her. Sarah looked into his eyes, angling her mouth better to receive his kiss.

Her mouth slightly parted, anticipating his kiss. His lips touched her softly, as if savoring every second, and a soft sigh escaped from her mouth giving him access. His tongue slowly met with hers in an erotic dance.

They could taste the wine they had, and each other's distinct taste. Caleb's hands moved to the back of Sarah's head and angled her head better to explore her mouth.

Sarah wanted skin. She wanted to feel his skin emanating heat as he caressed her mouth.

She pulled his shirt out of his jeans, and slid her hands under it and over the muscles on his back. She could feel his muscles tighten and release as she let her fingers glide, absorbing the heat from his body.

Caleb savored her touch. It was soft, hesitant and slightly inexperienced; it sent his hormones raging, his arousal growing with each touch. In a swift move, he picked her up and carried her over to the bed and set her down softly.

Sarah looked at him; her eyes had become indigo with arousal, her hair spread out on the bed cover. His chest tightened at the sight of her. She was offering him the night, and he was going to make the most it. With any other woman he would've been pumping by now, but something about Sarah made him want to savor every touch, every taste, every moment.

He wanted to take his time, his touch gentle. He pulled her shirt over her head and looked down at the simple cotton white bra. He had always preferred lace, and the more intricate female attires, but with Sarah he expected none of that and the simplicity of the cotton made him want her even more. Gently he unhooked the bra at the dip of her breasts, and slowly moved the cotton aside.

As his fingers grazed her breast, her body bucked in response. She was so responsive to his touch; Caleb wanted to cherish each response. His lips followed his fingers. He tasted, touched, explored. Her breath was short, sweat beading on her skin.

A fire blazed in her belly. A fire fuelled by desire for this man. At that moment Sarah knew of all the regrets she had in her life, and this would not be one of them. She offered her body to Caleb, relishing every touch accompanied by murmured words of appreciation.

She reached down to touch him. Experimentally her hand traced his steel length still trapped in his jeans, and Caleb's breath hitched. She needed Caleb tonight, and she could see the need reciprocated in his eyes as he reached up to feast on her mouth again. She pulled him towards her, her hips arching in response and let their combined needs take over.

Caleb collapsed on Sarah a few seconds after her body had drained his. "I wasn't expecting that."

Sarah laughed. "Neither was I, which was amazing." Caleb shifted off her, and she slowly started brushing the hair on his chest, "Is it always like that?" she asked shyly.

"Heavens, no," Caleb answered before thinking, until the meaning of her question along with her shy inexperienced touch dawned on him. "How many times have you made love with Grant?"

Sarah self-consciously turned away. "We tried it once, but it hurt and it was uncomfortable, after that we didn't try again."

Caleb ran his fingers through her hair. "The first time is meant to be sore, but if he had warmed you up nice and slow it would've been better."

A tear slid down Sarah's cheek. She thought of the opportunities and experiences she had missed following her parents expectations. "That's what I thought."

Caleb could hear the regret in her voice and slid his hand over her waist to the moist V at her thighs. "I can tell you one thing, Sarah Rothman, it was amazing, but you know what they say, practice makes perfect."

Sarah turned to look at him, disdain shining in her eyes. "Are you saying I need more practice?"

Caleb loved the way her temper flared. "Yes, I do. On one condition, I am the only one to teach you."

Catching the hint, Sarah giggled. "Well then, Mr. Sullivan, what did you have in mind?" She had just slept with a man she barely knew and yet she didn't feel the slightest hint of regret.

Caleb smiled and reached under the blanket; pouring fuel on to the embers of desire and relit the flames. The second time was faster, more urgent, and even better than the first time.

They lay talking and touching until eventually they succumbed to sleep. Through the night they reached for each other in a dream-like state, time and again before returning to sleep once more.

The patter of rain against the window woke Caleb. He thought of getting up, but that would mean moving Sarah, and she looked so restful he didn't have the heart to. She was draped over him. Her leg was arranged over both his legs; her head on his chest and her arm tucked around him. On second thought, he didn't want to move her.

Something was different; it had never felt like this before. Ever since Elizabeth's accident he knew he wouldn't ever be able to love again, but something about Sarah had his heart waking up from a long slumber. Every woman he had since knew that he left immediately, no soft words and no promises. But with Sarah something had changed. He wasn't sure what it was, but it made him uncomfortable. He wanted to spend time with her and get to know her even better. They had just spent the whole night making love, and he already wanted her again.

This was a recipe for disaster. It was better to hurt her now and make it clear that this was a onetime occurrence.

Sarah woke as she was pushed off Caleb. Rubbing the sleep from her eyes, she saw him dress with his back to her. Something was wrong. "Caleb?"

"I've got to go." He seemed angry and pissed off. "Thanks." He threw the word over his shoulder as he let himself out of the cottage.

Sarah was so stunned she didn't even reply. She wasn't so naive as to expect him to declare undying love to her after last night, but she also didn't expect him to run at the first sign of light. She couldn't stop the first tear that slipped down her cheek and swiftly brushed it off; mad at herself for feeling too much.

She couldn't allow herself to feel something for him. He could at least have waited for her to wake up enough not to be shocked by his departure. Even though he claimed that he had never cheated, Sarah wasn't sure the treatment she had just received was much better. She didn't want a relationship, she didn't need one.

Her father's betrayal rang clear in her mind. How would she be able to ever trust a man, when the one she had trusted completely lived a lie? After he had used her trust in him to manipulate her into becoming someone she wasn't?

Though she knew before inviting Caleb to stay that it wouldn't be anything more than one night, his touch, his kisses, had made her feel special. Now she felt discarded, used and cheap.

She made her way to the shower and tried not to think of all the ways he had touched her, the caresses that made her beg for more.

No one could've been a kinder lover to re-introduce her to the art of love making; she was certain of that. But that was over now. If it hadn't been for the storm, the wine and the candlelight, it would probably never have happened.

She would put it aside and remember why she came to Blue Hill in the first place. To find herself, not a man. Especially not one as complicated as Caleb. She took her time getting ready and then headed over to the main house to start on the day's chores. Hopefully that would keep her busy enough to not think of Caleb or what happened between them.

"There's nothing in the pantry?" Caleb accused Sarah as he walked into the dining room of the main house where she was unpacking the silver cutlery later that morning.

"You were supposed to be here for breakfast, tomorrow is pantry basket day," Sarah stated caustically as she wiped down the silver.

"Fine, I'll get something in town."

"Don't bother, I kept your breakfast hot, it's in the heat tray of the oven."

She didn't even bother to look up at him. She couldn't allow him to see how hurt she was after how he left this morning. She wanted to appear cool and unattached as the women he was used to seeing, but Sarah found it very hard.

"Thanks," he said as he turned to head to the kitchen.

He opened the warm tray and found a cooked farm breakfast. The eggs had gone rubbery, but the bacon was still crisp and the sausage delightfully juicy. He had expected her to say something, he mused as he took the first bite.

He was thrown off balance by the fact that she didn't. Didn't last night have the same effect on her? Not that it mattered to him, he lied to himself. Why did it bother him so much? It's not like he cared. A niggling thought in the back of his mind suggested she might be the one woman he'd like to stay, and she might be the one who wouldn't.

He would take some time later to ponder on the foreign feelings that were taking hold in his heart. For now he needed to focus on a dark forest where a girl lay wounded, violated and praying for a quick death.

The Cahills' were a bubbly pair of pensioners who came to Oak Cottages every year before winter set in. This was their fifth visit and they were disappointed to find Gladys wasn't there, but they enjoyed their young hostess's personality and her eagerness to listen to stories that had already been reminisced about to everyone they knew.

Oak Cottages was their annual romantic weekend. Their dates rarely changed, and the number of nights didn't.

Bride on the Run

They always stayed for two nights, spending their days alone, and their evenings with Gladys who had become a dear friend.

Sarah enjoyed their company. On the first night they invited her to have dinner with them, saying they could always have dinner alone at home.

The evening was a jovial event. The Cahills' spoke about their grandchildren back in South Dakota, about their family farm and told her the story of how they fell in love fifty years ago against all odds. The farmer's daughter and the farm hand. Sarah enjoyed talking to them, laughing with them, and envied their relationship with each other.

They were comfortable with each other, finishing each other's sentences, not in a way that seemed to interrupt, but in a way that seemed to complete. Luckily they didn't ask anything about Sarah she didn't willingly offer.

After Sarah had bid them goodnight and made sure the main house was secured for the night, she made her way to her cottage. She was bone tired after working all day, on her feet for most of it. She loved the feeling. She had made a difference in the Cahills' day.

She wasn't just idly sipping ice tea and attending ladies lunches, discussing the latest shade of eye shadow or designer purse. She wondered what her mother would've thought of her cleaning and running a tourist establishment.

A smile crossed her face as she could imagine the appalled look on her mother's face.

Stepping into the dark cottage, she glanced around as she switched on the lights. Avoiding looking at the bed, she chastened herself for thinking of Caleb and how he had made her feel in it.

Pushing those thoughts aside, she took a quick shower and slipped under the covers. The day had taken its toll and luckily she drifted into sleep swiftly, but she couldn't chase away the dreams of Caleb as easily.

The next morning Sarah was up early, after a night of tossing and turning. She headed over to the main house, and started on breakfast for the Cahills'.

For Caleb's pantry basket, she baked some fresh muffins, grateful that Gladys had a cookbook in the kitchen, labeled with the precise instructions for all the baked confectionaries she made for her guests.

She packed Caleb's basket with fresh poppy seed and lemon muffins, fresh squeezed orange juice, ham and Swiss cheese sandwiches and some cold meats, and placed thoughts of him along with the basket in the pantry.

The rest of day was filled with chores and cleaning, and she had just sat down to make a grocery list when the phone rang; as she glanced down she recognized the number, grateful for the interruption from Gladys. "Hi, Gladys," Sarah answered the phone.

"Hello, dear, how are you?"

"Fine, the Cahills' are very happy, and Oak Cottages are still standing," Sarah laughed.

"Thank you, Sarah, I really appreciate it, which makes me hesitant to ask more of you."

"Not at all. If you need to stay a few days more to take care of your sister, don't worry about Oak Cottages."

"Not a few days, Sarah," Gladys sighed. "A few months at least."

"Oh dear, how is she doing?"

"It seems the stroke affected all her motor functions. They're releasing her home, but only if I can stay with her. She'll need help bathing, and eating and she can't speak properly, so it's best if it's done by someone she is comfortable with."

Sarah let the news sink in. This was a large responsibility, but she wasn't going to disappoint Gladys. "Gladys, don't worry, I'll take care of Oak Cottages for you. I figured out how the reservation system works and we only have a few more bookings till the end of the month when we close for winter."

"Are you sure, dear? That's a lot of work for one person."

"I'm fine, I'm enjoying it tremendously. I have to admit I might make a copy of the recipe book you keep in the kitchen. It seems every recipe just works perfectly."

"I'm glad someone appreciates it. I always thought I was going through all the trouble for nothing setting it out so detailed."

"I appreciate it. And really, I'll cope." Sarah opened up the reservation screen on the computer in front of her and saw there were quite a few bookings for the next month, but none overlapping, which meant she would at most have two people to host at a time, excluding Caleb.

"How's Caleb doing?" Gladys enquired.

"He's fine, hibernating; I haven't seen much of him." Sarah thanked the heavens that Gladys couldn't see the tell-tale blush on her face at that moment.

"I feel horrible leaving you with him. He might still be there when I get back. Are you sure you're alright with this, I wouldn't want his moods to make you uncomfortable."

If only Gladys knew. "Don't worry, we figured out a schedule for cleaning and eating that suits his writing."

"Hopefully I'll be home before December," Gladys pondered. "How long are you planning on staying, Sarah, I wouldn't want to impose on your plans."

"As long as you need me, Gladys. Take care of your sister." Sarah thought for a moment, and then added, "I'm in no rush to go back to Savannah."

"Thank you, Sarah." Gladys went onto explain to Sarah where the keys to the safe were, and said Sarah should use the cash for supplies, groceries and incidentals. She trusted Sarah to look after repairs if something should pop up. "If you send me your banking details, I'll start depositing a weekly wage for you; you're doing much more now than earning room and board."

Sarah laughed. "Don't worry about that right now; we'll sort something out when you get back."

"All right, but if you need money you phone me."

"I'm sure that won't be necessary, but I'll keep it in mind."

"Thank you so much, Sarah."

"It's my pleasure, take care." Sarah hung up the phone. She didn't want to go into the details with Gladys of why she wasn't using her bank account. Her father could too easily find her then. She still had enough cash to tide her over until Gladys got back.

She started making some scones for the Cahills' and once they were in the oven; she raided the pantry for a selection of jellies. Setting a tray with the jellies, scones, cheese and tea, she carried it out to the Cahills' where they were relaxing on the front veranda of the main house. Finding them deep in conversation, Sarah set the tray down, advised them what time dinner would be and excused herself.

Having some time before she needed to prepare dinner, she headed over to her cottage and grabbed her art supplies and went down to the beach to set up her easel.

The salty sea breeze licked at her face. There was a chill in the air, warning winter approached earlier in Maine. With the surf breaking a few yards away and the gulls flying overhead, Sarah started to paint.

She found herself pouring her battling emotions, her heartache and her feelings for Caleb into her art. She set a timer on her watch making sure she didn't lose track; she couldn't let the Cahills' go hungry on account of her painting.

She began by whimsically brushing long topaz strokes across the canvas to emphasize the different colors of blue the sky had to offer, and lost herself in shading and blending.

A while later, as she sat back and looked at the canvas in front of her, Sarah realized something without guilt for the first time. She could really paint. Not knowing if it was her emotions, her need to express herself or her talent, she was astonished at what she had just created. She did have talent, and she wouldn't ever deny herself of her art again. She'd be able to sell this.

With a thought blooming in her mind, she started thinking of what she would prepare for dinner.

Chapter 10

THE following afternoon after the Cahills' had left and the chores had been done, Sarah got into her grey sedan. She had mustered all her courage and had placed some of her paintings on the backseat. She stopped at the local art supply store she visited after just arriving in Blue Hill.

After a bit of negotiating and accepting due praise from the proprietor, they agreed Sarah would be able to sell her art there. Sarah was ecstatic. She was going to sell her art. She felt proud of herself, a foreign emotion, one she normally only sought from her parents. She had accomplished something without her father pulling strings, or her mother objecting. She would see how quickly her paintings sold, but at this stage she needed four more to display.

As Sarah drove back to Oak Cottages she was elated. She stopped at the liquor store and bought champagne. Tonight she would cook a meal for herself and celebrate her achievement with bubbly. To anyone else this might've appeared sad, but to Sarah it symbolized her first step to independence, away from Savannah society.

She grabbed her easel and paint, riding on the waves of achievement and headed to the kitchen. She had always wanted to try a still life of a fruit basket, tonight she would indulge herself. She would paint, drink champagne and cook for herself.

Caleb's stomach growled, alerting him to the time of day. It was already dark outside; he hadn't even been to the main house to collect his pantry basket. He grabbed a sweater from the back of the door and headed towards the main house on the small walkway.

The dark cloud still hung over him from the words he wrote that day. As he neared the back door he could hear Alanis Morissette saying her thanks, and the fragrant smell of Cajun spices. He cracked open the door slowly, hesitant to interrupt if there were guests. What he found in the kitchen caused a slow smile to spread across his face, and the dark cloud lifted for the first time in weeks.

Caleb watched her without alerting her to his presence. She had so many facets to her personality he would've liked to explore, if only he knew he wouldn't hurt her. She was sitting at an easel painting a fruit basket stationed on the kitchen island. Her hair was loose, falling strands of woven gold across her back. She was singing along to the music as if she had written the lyrics herself. The delicious smell came from a pot that was simmering on the stove. It hinted at spice and variety; curious about the content, and for the woman behind the easel, he eased to door open.

As if sensing she was being watched, the hairs at the back of Sarah's neck stood up. The cold air blowing in hinted that the back door was open. She stopped singing and slowly turned around to find Caleb watching her from the open door.

She was celebrating and didn't feel up to playing cat and mouse games with him tonight, especially not after the way he ran from her bed the day before.

"Do you need something?" she asked with raised eyebrows, not bothering to put down the brush or to get up.

"Just collecting my basket," he answered with a smile still tugging at the corners of his mouth.

"In the pantry." She turned back to her easel and continued to paint, but didn't sing this time.

Caleb noticed her shoulders tense at the sight of him, and didn't understand why he wanted to apologize for yesterday. Ever since Elizabeth had passed, he didn't even wait for the sheets to cool before leaving whenever he sought out a woman for night.

The fact that he wanted to stay with Sarah and allowed himself to fall asleep, had caught him off guard, and he didn't know how to handle that. Or the fact that just seeing her had his system buzzing with want again.

He thought having her would fulfill the need. But he already wanted her again, needed to feel her writhe and moan beneath him.

He walked over to the pantry; opened the door and picked up the basket. "Goodnight," he said as he headed for the door.

Sarah put down her brush and stood up. "This is stupid, Caleb," she said, throwing her hands in the air. "Yes, we slept together, yes, you were a dick about it, but do we really have to spend the following months treating each other as polite strangers, with this cloud of shame hovering? For heaven's sake, I was under the impression we were two consenting adults?"

Caleb was startled by her direct approach, and was temporarily at a loss for words. "Uh …"

"Typical, exactly what I thought would happen; you can't even look me in the eye. Breakfast is at nine tomorrow morning." Sarah shook her head, picked up her brush and continued to paint.

Caleb knew she was giving him out for yesterday morning, and searched for a neutral subject to change the atmosphere. "Celebrating?" he asked as his eye caught the champagne.

"As a matter of fact I am," Sarah answered reticently, her back still turned to him.

"Care to enlighten me?"

She understood this was the closest to an apology she was going to get, so allowed him to change the subject. "The Art Supply Store slash Gallery in town agreed to display some of my paintings."

"Wow, congratulations, I told you that you were good ..."

"Thanks, I know, but it's different coming from the proprietor of an art store. He will be taking a percentage of each sale, and will only stock five pieces at a time, but he's willing to give me chance."

"I've been in there a few times, and their standards are quite high. I think your paintings are going to do really well."

Sarah smiled at the backwards compliment; even if he was a complete pain in the rear, at least he believed in her.

Caleb set the basket down on the kitchen island a small distance from her fruit basket. "What's on the stove, it smells delicious."

"Jambalaya." Sarah dipped her brush into a moss green blob on her palette and started on outlining what seemed to be the beginnings of an avocado pear. "I had a taste for the south this evening."

"Isn't that just a gooey concoction of chicken, shrimp and sausage?" Caleb asked, pulling his face in distaste.

"As a matter of fact it is, and after you had one bite, you'll be turning that frown upside down." She waved her brush at him.

"Are you inviting me to dinner?" Caleb flirted easily and immediately almost kicked himself under the table as Sarah's eyes shot up to meet his.

"I'm not inviting you to anything, but you're more than welcome to some, it'll be ready in about fifteen minutes. If you like you can have a glass of champagne while you wait," Sarah answered evenly.

Caleb walked over to the glass-fronted cupboard where the champagne glasses were kept, and poured some for him. As he sat down, he admired Sarah's painting skill. He wasn't an expert, but he could appreciate talent when he saw it.

"How long have you been painting?"

Sarah laughed dryly. "According to my mother, only during classes while I was at college." She took a sip of champagne, savoring the taste of the bubbles as they exploded with flavor against the roof of her mouth. "But in truth, every time I had a chance since middle school."

"Doesn't your mother want you to paint?" Caleb asked.

"Oh, she did, as long as she didn't know about it, have to look at it, and it didn't interfere with my wedding to Grant." Sarah shrugged briefly before a fierce smile lighted up the room. "And that's why it's so exciting for me to be able to display my paintings."

"It seems to me you're enjoying your rebellion."

"Rebellion, discovering myself, enlightenment, call it what you like, but at least I'm calling the shots."

"Fair enough."

"How's the book going?" Sarah asked after a few minutes of silence. He wasn't a torrid bull tonight, but she could still see the shadows under his eyes.

"Still in the dark," Caleb answered. "When is Gladys coming back?" Caleb swiftly redirected, indicating he wasn't going to expand on the subject.

"She actually phoned today," Sarah said as she started putting away her palette and inks. "She'll hopefully be back before December, but her sister experienced quite a setback from the stroke and she'll need to stay longer to take care of her."

"I'm sorry to hear that. Will Oak Cottages be closing now?" Caleb asked.

"No, we only have a few bookings left before closing for winter next month, and I offered to handle them for her."

"That's very kind of you."

Her nerves sprang to attention. Caleb was being agreeable and kind; he hadn't been this way since the first night he arrived at Oak Cottages, and she was afraid he was going to turn into Mr. Hyde any moment now. Or she was going to succumb, again.

"Not really. I was planning on staying for another couple of months, so this way I'll have something to do as well."

A heady smell started drifting through the kitchen indicating the Jambalaya was simmered through.

"And once Oak Cottages closes in a month, are you going to use that time to paint?"

"Yes," Sarah answered as she reached in a high cupboard to retrieve plates.

Caleb couldn't help but appreciate at how well her jean hugged her behind. With her top sliding up, he had a glimpse of soft skin, and for a moment remembered what it was like to glide his lips and hands over that skin.

Sarah turned, meeting Caleb's eyes; she could see where his thoughts had gone. Unable to stop herself, she thought of walking over to him and kissing him, wanting to find out if that want was still burning for him too.

Clearing her head of the thought, she broke eye contact and headed to the stove.

She set Caleb's plate in front of him without looking at him, afraid she wouldn't be able to control her own urges.

As Caleb took the first bite he couldn't stop the moans of satisfaction emanating from his throat. It was sweet and sour and spicy all at the same time. The buttery chicken, with the chewy sausage complemented the array of vegetables so completely; he couldn't understand how people could not enjoy it.

Sarah grinned with satisfaction; he was thoroughly relishing the jambalaya. Raising an eyebrow, she prompted, "I guess the concoction isn't that bad?"

He only grunted as he continued chewing.

After a few bites he asked enthusiastically, "Where on earth did you learn to cook like that? I guess not at debutante school?"

Sarah gave a laugh. "Our Creole cook." Sipping champagne, she continued, "Whenever I wanted to hide out from my overbearing mother, I would go to the kitchen, knowing that was the one place in the house she never went."

"At this moment I'm very grateful you needed a place to hide out."

"I loved it," Sarah reminisced fondly. "Cook didn't mind if I got dirty, how I pronounced my vowels, or what I was wearing. She taught me, amongst other things, how to make perfect southern fried chicken, bake bread and, of course, make Jambalaya."

"Did you ever bother eating anything else?" he asked incredulously.

"I think you're mistaken, Mr. Sullivan. This slaver's fare would never be served in our dining room in Savannah. This was only cooked for the help. I ate this in the kitchen along with cook and the servants."

After a second helping and some more light conversation, Caleb stood up. "Well, I'm off to bed." As soon as he said the words, the air grew thick with temptation.

Green eyes met blue, unanswered questions were seeking answers in their depths, neither wanting to break the contact. Sweetness floated on the air. Temptation hung in the balance.

Sarah instinctively crossed her hands across her chest, trying to stop her heart from yearning for his touch.

Caleb noticed and knew that if he wanted he could have her right now; she was nervous and she wanted him. He felt his groin respond. Her cheeks flushed crimson. A magnetic pull was forcing them to say something, do something, but neither wanted to be the first to concede. Caleb occupied his hands by picking up the pantry basket.

He wanted to step closer, to kiss her and hold her, but he couldn't allow that. He needed distance from the feelings he was having.

Sarah was having trouble remembering what he had just said and how to answer. Her feelings mirrored his, she wanted him, but she couldn't allow herself to fall in love with a man she couldn't trust.

Caleb walked towards her slowly, gripping the basket until his knuckles were white with effort. He knew if he put the basket down now, he wouldn't be able to control his hands or his urges. As if he was in a dream he bent down to kiss her, his lips inches away from hers, her breath on his skin, their eyes drowning in each other.

After what felt like an eternity Caleb turned his mouth to brush her cheek with his lips. With a voice like rough gravel, he said, "I'm sorry." He broke eye contact, and left.

Chapter 11

THE following weeks flew by in a blur of guests, housekeeping, cooking and keeping the pantry stocked for Caleb. Breakfast conversation with Caleb was usually few and far between.

He came, he ate, he left. He was deeply involved with his writing, and Sarah never asked how the book was progressing - she could tell from his state of mind. She never saw him on the days she left him a pantry basket.

She spent what little free time she had painting. Her first paintings sold within a week, and the boost of confidence allowed Sarah to be more experimental; she tried new techniques, and relished the time spent with her inks and canvasses. When she went back to Savannah no one could ever stop her from painting again. The paintings weren't selling for much as she was a new artist, but it was enough to keep her cash float healthy.

It was early November and winter was fast approaching. Sarah was grateful for the amount of inspiration she had from the leaves changing color during the past month. Her landscapes of northern Maine were filled with rich autumn hues, clear blue waters and numerous sunsets over the fall colors. They had sold the quickest, but she had kept one, to remind herself of her time in Blue Hill.

With the icy fingers of winter reaching out, the symphony of colors receded. The rich hues that once enticed her, had now become eerie forests, ghostlike trees with branch arms reaching toward the skies. No one would ever be able to take this time away from her.

Sarah looked forward to Oak Cottages closing at the end of the week. There weren't any reservations for the remainder of the week, but she had received quite a few last minute bookings in the past month, so she had learned to be prepared for guests at all times.

The days Oak Cottages had no guests except for Caleb, she drove until she found a landscape that called to her. She had left a note on the front door of the main house, instructing any guests to leave a number and she'd phone them back on her return. She had gotten two bookings on one day with her last note, and didn't leave Oak Cottages again for fear of losing business.

She spoke with Gladys at least once a week regarding the running of Oak Cottages; her sister was doing better, but Gladys wouldn't be able to return before December. Sarah still thought about Caleb every day and not just about what she had to cook for him or pack in his pantry basket, but in trying to comprehend the feelings she was having. She was irritated with his foul mood, but at the same time empathetic for what he was going through alone in that cabin.

Sarah had read one of his books back in Savannah, and she could still recall the vivid way he described the crimes. She couldn't help but imagine what it would be like to know him when he wasn't writing.

She tried to make light conversation on the mornings he came to breakfast, even though he barely spoke. She could feel him watching her when she prepared his breakfast. His presence still gave her butterflies and the air seemed to thicken with sexual attraction whenever they were alone.

Today was pantry basket day, and yet the basket was still in the pantry though it was nearing dinner time.

Sarah fixed herself some toasted ham, cheese and tomato sandwiches and headed over to her cottage. She wouldn't make the mistake of taking him food again. She fell asleep late night with a book on her chest, snuggled under the covers with the embers radiating heat from the fireplace.

It felt like minutes later when a knocking at her door waked her. She stood up and grabbed a robe and pulled it on, and headed for the door. She didn't know what to expect, but she didn't expect to find Caleb looking worn and tired, on her doorstep in the middle of the night.

"Are you okay?" she asked carefully.

"I will be; the worst part is over."

He didn't know why he was there knocking her awake at 2 a.m. He didn't understand the need to be with her tonight, but when the serial killer was arrested by the FBI and he closed the chapter, he needed to see her. For the first time Caleb felt he needed someone to help him escape the darkness.

Sarah took a moment to understand what he meant. "Do you need anything?" She knew she shouldn't be asking, or offering help. She should distance herself from him.

"Yes, let me come in, Sarah, I want to hold you. I need to hold you."

This was a broken man standing in front of her, a man hurting, asking her for comfort. She couldn't turn him away, her heart ached for him. Ignoring all the warnings in her mind, her heart yearned for him.

She opened the door wider; she dropped the robe over the sofa couch and got into bed.

Opening the covers, she invited him in. He kicked off his shoes and clothes and got into bed with only his boxer. He turned around and took her in his arms. Sarah expected him to make love to her. She was wrong. He needed comfort. He was holding her so tight it almost hurt. She had never seen a man so vulnerable before and felt privileged to witness it, to help soothe, to be needed.

She fell asleep in his arms, dreaming of belonging to this Jekyll and Hyde.

The next morning Sarah woke first. She got up quickly and moved towards the en suite bathroom; she didn't want to be there when Caleb pulled his disappearing act again.

She'd rather have her shower and find the cottage empty when she was done. Somehow, sleeping with him, in his arms, had been more intimate to her than making love.

They had slept in perfect sync, when the one turned, the other followed. Holding on to each other, reaching for each other. She wouldn't be able to handle his anger this morning. She turned the shower on, undressed and stepped in. She hummed a country song about losing your mind when you lost your heart, and started washing her hair. Just when she was sure she *had* lost her mind, the shower curtain was pulled back and Caleb stepped in.

"Good morning." He kissed her cheek and took her in his arms for a wet hug.

Sarah didn't know how to react. It seemed like he was out of his miserable stint, but she waited for confirmation before speaking. She smiled at him as she continued soaping her hair.

"I guess you'd like an explanation for last night."

"It's not really a habit of mine to invite guests into my bed when they knock me awake in the middle of the night," she started building a lather of shampoo in her hair as she looked at him, " but it looked like you needed it."

"I finished the worst part, from here on its collecting and presenting evidence, the court case, etc." His hands reached for her hair and helped her rinse the soap suds from it. "I've only known you for a little more than a month, but last night I realized for the first time I couldn't escape it on my own, I needed you." His voice was sincere as their eyes met.

Sarah realized the gravity of his confession. "How did you normally escape it?"

"Whiskey, bottles and bottles." He gave a wry laugh. "I poured myself a glass last night, and realized I needed you more than the whiskey."

Her defenses were crumbling. His confession was honesty calling to the honesty she so badly wanted. Not ready to chance her heart, she answered him coyly, "Caleb, I'm glad I could help last night, but I'm not looking for a relationship."

"That's my line, Sarah." He ran his hands down her back and skimmed her behind. "Now I know what it feels like to be on the receiving side. It sucks."

Caleb brushed his fingers over her breast and teased them to harden to his touch. She was so responsive and he wanted nothing more right now than to take her hot and fast.

Sarah could feel the need pooling between her legs - how could her body betray her like this?

She savored the feel of his hands on her naked body. Her hips bucked in response to his teasing, but he wouldn't put out the fire of desire. His hands were clever, teasing. His mouth feasted on her neck. Sarah reached out and touched the taut muscles on his chest. She wanted to feel him respond to her. His lips trailed down, suckling on her breast.

On a hitched breath, she moaned, "Caleb, you're playing dirty."

"Actually, I think I'm playing really clean."

Sarah laughed before she said, "I'm serious, Caleb, and I've got too much to figure out. I won't be able to trust anyone until I've come to terms with my family."

"I'll help you," came his quick answer. Leaving the softness of her breasts, he kissed her mouth softly, enticingly. "Not all men cheat, Sarah, not all men manipulate. Give me a chance to prove that to you," he said in barely more than whisper.

"Let me think on it first." Having an affair with Caleb would be wonderful, but she knew eventually he would let her down, and hurt her, or she would start being what *he* needed. And from now on she fully intended on only being herself. But how could she stop this need pooling, the fire burning.

She reached for him and on a sigh said, "For now just touch me."

Caleb smiled slowly. "It would be my pleasure."

His hands explored, teased and made her weak with want. Sarah indulged herself by kissing his neck, tasting soap, water and Caleb. Unable to contain his need any longer Caleb picked her up and lost himself in her.

They stepped out of the shower stall and started toweling themselves dry, when Caleb pulled her towards him and feasting on her mouth again.

"How about this? Take today to think things over and tomorrow evening we have dinner."

"Like a date?" Sarah asked suspiciously, as her fingers combed through his wet hair.

"Exactly like a date," Caleb said, giving her a light smack on the bum.

"I'm not sure, Caleb." Sarah answered, slapping his hand away.

"Just think about it. I'd like to tell you something. Let's talk tomorrow night?" He looked at her with the question in his eyes.

"Alright, but that means no knocking me awake in the middle of the night."

"Don't worry," he smiled. "After the dark part is done, I normally take a few days off to relax. So you don't even have to see me today or tomorrow, I'll take care of my own meals." He winked at her as he stepped out of the small bathroom.

Seconds later Sarah heard the cottage door click close behind him.

Chapter 12

SARAH started unpacking the groceries; the afternoon light was streaming through the window of the kitchen reflecting the lightness of her mood. She had spent all of yesterday getting up to date with the chores around Oak Cottages and today she took for herself.

She spent the morning playing around with an idea for a painting. When she had finished, she was satisfied with the result. She had painted Caleb. His face grinned back at her like he did when he was in a good mood. The likeness of the painting had Sarah feeling proud of her attempt.

Afterwards she spoiled herself with a haircut and a facial. She wanted a shorter cut, easier to maintain herself, and opted for a shoulder length bob. She tried to convince herself she wasn't going through all the trouble for Caleb, but in her heart she knew the truth. She didn't know what he wanted to tell her, maybe he was an axe murderer, and maybe he was leaving, but when she woke up this morning, she decided she'd give him tonight.

Southern fried chicken with vegetables, yes; she would cook that, and serve him some chardonnay. Even though she was looking forward to it, she was still hesitant, knowing that she lost all perspective when he touched her. She wondered if he was going to be charming, kind or rude.

She'd come to understand the reason for his rudeness. That didn't mean she enjoyed him being rude, but somehow that made him seem more real to her.

Preparing the chicken, she thought of her parents. She couldn't remember her mother cooking a meal for them once in her life; yes, the odd sandwich, or microwave popcorn. She wondered if all women enjoyed cooking for the men they loved …

Sarah stopped mid-thought.

Did she say love? She couldn't be in love with Caleb. She still had to talk to Grant, face her father, forgive her mother; she couldn't be falling in love in Maine.

Thrown off balance by her revelation, Sarah immersed herself in the cooking, focusing on the flavors, the batter and spices.

When Caleb stepped into the kitchen at six o'clock, she was still rattled with the thoughts of being in love.

Her eyes flew to him briefly before returning her focus to frying the chicken.

She didn't want to look at him directly, for fear he saw what she felt in her eyes.

"Are you going to open the wine for us, I'm almost done here," Sarah said nervously.

Caleb picked up on Sarah's nerves; she was strung as tight as guitar chord. "Sure," he said easily. He poured them each a glass. "How was your day?" He set the glass in front of her next to the cooker.

"Fine." Sarah took a sip of chardonnay and tried to balance her emotions with neutral conversation. "I dropped off more canvasses. They're actually selling quite well."

"I'm glad for you." Caleb sat down at the kitchen island. "I need to run a few errands in town tomorrow if you'd like to grab the cleaning supplies and attack my cottage."

Sarah laughed, "I think I'll need to cart the heavy duty supplies out of the shed for that."

"It's not that bad, I clean."

Sarah raised her brows at his statement.

"Okay, I don't clean, but I do rinse the sink after I shave, and I kick the mud off my boots before going inside," he said triumphantly.

Sarah laughed; this was the jovial Caleb that kissed her the first time.

This would make tonight so much harder. It was hard not to fall in love with someone who caused electric currents to run through your system at a mere touch, and made you laugh with abandon.

"Heavy duty supplies it is," Sarah confirmed with a teasing smile.

"You changed your hair," Caleb stated.

Sarah touched it self-consciously. "Yes, I felt like a change."

"It suits you better than the long locks."

He looked at her in way that had heat crawling into her cheeks; she turned back to the cooker.

They chatted amicably while she was preparing dinner. When Sarah served the fried chicken, Caleb was convinced the Colonel got his recipe from her.

After dinner the atmosphere grew leaden with expectation, it was time to talk.

"So what did you want to tell me?" Sarah asked carefully.

"Right." Caleb wiped his hands on a napkin and folded his hands in front of him. "I was also engaged to be married."

"Did you also run?" Sarah teased.

"No, she died," Caleb said in somber tone of voice.

Nearly biting her tongue for her callous comment, she asked, concerned, "What happened?"

Caleb laced his fingers and twiddled his thumbs, focusing intently on his hands as he started telling her about Elizabeth. "We were young, and in love. Everyone was against the wedding at our age, we were barely twenty-one, but we knew we were meant for each other. It was that once in a lifetime type of love."

Caleb looked out the window into the darkness searching for words to describe that feeling to Sarah.

"You can't sleep, you can't eat, it's like every breath depends on knowing that she is all right." He took a sip of his wine, and continued. "I started writing my first book, Elizabeth worked long hours trying to prove herself at a new job. One night she was working late, I was supposed to go and fetch her, but Elizabeth knew I was in the middle of an important chapter and insisted she was fine to drive, and she had her car at work, she'd be home soon."

Caleb pressed his fingers to his eyes; he could still feel the pain.

"When the phone rang, I immediately knew something was wrong. Call it instinct, I don't know. I just knew. It was her parents. A drunk driver ran a red light and smashed into her. She died on impact."

He took a deep breath to steady himself.

"Caleb, I'm so sorry," Sarah said empathetically as she reached across the counter to hold his hand.

"I blamed myself, some days I still do. The medical examiner, her parents, my parents, all tried to make me see it wasn't my fault. But if I hadn't been so wrapped up in my writing, I would've taken better care of her."

Sarah didn't say anything. She understood what he meant and, if he wasn't going to believe his family and the medical examiner, nothing she could say would make a difference.

She waited for him to continue.

"The day of Elizabeth's funeral, her sister had a mental breakdown. She was always very fragile, apparently there were complications at birth, and Elizabeth's death seemed to overwhelm her. She blamed me; I could see it in her eyes. Our parents are still friends, which makes it harder to know that her sister still hasn't recovered completely from the breakdown."

"I'm sorry to hear that, Caleb."

"To me it feels like I let Elizabeth die because I couldn't take care of her and because of that I ruined her sister's life."

"Caleb, she was hurt and confused needed a fall guy, that doesn't make it your fault." Sarah shook her head. "You can't take the blame for this."

"Like I said, most days I don't. But since then I've never allowed myself to fall in love again. I know with my writing I'll let the person in my life down, and honestly I didn't think I still had it in me to love someone that much. It was like she took a piece of my heart with her to heaven."

The kitchen was quiet for a long time, until Sarah said, "I think if you lose someone you love, that piece of your heart isn't gone, it will just always be occupied by the love and the memories of the person you love."

Caleb looked up at her, searching her eyes for a way to tell her how he felt. "That's why I've been rude and miserable and avoiding you." He took Sarah's hands in his own. "It feels like you've started to make more room in my heart, I wasn't sure I wanted you to."

Sarah was stunned by his confession; never could she have dreamed this was what he was going to say to her tonight.

"Caleb …"

"Wait," he held up his hand, "let me finish. I never thought I could feel like this again. I wasn't looking for it, and I definitely wasn't expecting it. All I'm asking is, give us, give this a chance."

"I don't know what to say. I wasn't expecting this, touché." She gave a wry laugh.

"But?" Caleb knew there was 'but' coming.

"But I have nothing to offer you; I have to work through my trust issues."

"Let me work through them with you, don't let your family keep you from being happy." Caleb stood and briskly started pacing. "If you can tell me right now that you don't feel anything for me, that you can go the rest of your life without regretting giving us a chance, I'll walk away this moment. You won't ever have to see me again."

Sarah shook her head and couldn't stop the tear escaping from her eye. "I do feel something for you, but I'm afraid."

"Afraid of what?"

"Afraid I won't be able to be myself, afraid I won't be able to trust you, and afraid I'll get hurt."

"Sarah, we all get hurt, it's taken me years to recover from the hurt of losing Elizabeth, but I'll never regret loving her, it made me a better person. I never knew I could feel this way again and yet somehow it's better."

He smiled at her with that charm he rarely doled out. "It's that can't sleep, can't eat, can't breathe feeling."

"You'd make a good lawyer." She looked him straight in the eye. "I'm willing to see where this goes, no promises, for as long as we're Oak Cottages. I need to stay at least until Gladys gets back, which gives us a month."

"I'll take a month," Caleb said and then continued with self-assurance, "I'll need less than a month to convince you." He leaned across the table and kissed her. "I have another favor to ask of you."

"Okay?" Sarah answered carefully. She wasn't sure how much she would be able to offer him on one night.

"I've never let anyone read my work before I send it to my editor, but I'd like to share it with you. Would you be interested in reading it?"

Sarah understood this was almost as hard for him as admitting he had feelings for her. She knew he was a good writer, and what an honor it would be to read his work.

"I'll be honored." Sarah smiled and Caleb leaned in for another kiss. She let him tease the seam of her lips open. "You're very sure of yourself, C.B. Sullivan," she said between kisses.

He stood up and moved around the counter, not letting go of her hands. As he reached her he took her face in his hands. "Let me love you tonight," he said as he looked into her eyes.

Sarah pulled away from him and headed for the kitchen door, and Caleb felt his world fall apart as she walked away.

Chapter 13

"**ONLY** if you can catch me." Sarah turned at the door with a challenge in her eyes, a smile spreading, and sprinted towards her cottage.

It took Caleb a moment to comprehend what she meant, before he took off after her. His long strides chewed up the path between them; he reached her just as she reached the steps of her cottage. Short of breath, she turned to look at him smiling, daring him to do something. He grabbed her by the waist and threw her over his shoulder in a fireman's lift; he carried her into the cottage and set her down.

"I ought to spank you for making my heart jump in my throat like that."

Sarah giggled, she didn't know this side of her, this person she was when she was with Caleb, and she was starting to like it.

Not being experienced in making love, she didn't know what to do next, but she wanted to at least try to seduce Caleb.

She moved her hands towards his belt and started undoing the buckle. Caleb's breath hitched as she pulled his shirt out of his trousers and her hands met skin. She looked up at him for some sort of confirmation that she wasn't doing anything wrong. His eyes were half closed, stormy green irises watching her under thick black lashes.

Her hands slid up his arms to his shoulders and entwined themselves in the unruly hair at his nape; she stood on her toes to meet his lips with her own.

Caleb realized what she was doing, and let her. Every woman needed to know the power she had over a man that wanted her, the power to entice reactions in his body, to make his eyes go glaze over with lust.

He didn't know how long he'd be able to let her, but for now he enjoyed every second. Sarah started kissing him softly, but the kiss soon turned to hunger for each other when their tongues starting dueling an age old rhythm. She let her hands trail down his back over his lean muscles, and reached under his shirt. She pulled it up inch by inch, not losing momentum in the kiss.

When finally the shirt reached his shoulders, Caleb swiftly pulled it over his head. He watched her, waiting for her next move. She started undoing the buttons on her shirt, and when she reached the last one she let her shirt drop to the floor. She was wearing a white lace bra, her dark brown nipples straining against the fabric.

Watching Caleb's eyes on her body, she felt bolder and started to undo her jeans, very, very slowly.

Caleb didn't realize he was holding his breath.

He watched as she slowly shimmied out the dark blue fabric, she stepped out of them with slim pale legs; her Savannah tan had faded in the time she'd been in Blue Hill.

Sarah met his eyes as she undid the clasp of her bra behind her back, and by the time the falling lace touched the floor, Caleb already had her on the bed.

Bliss.

It was the only word that could describe the feeling of knowing Caleb was in love with her and waking up in his arms.

Their continuous love making during the night had left marks on her body and she ached in places she didn't know she had muscles, and she loved it. Knowing that Caleb knew her away from the farce of the society she was part of and still wanted her, gave her satisfaction.

He knew the real Sarah. Not the one that always talked and walked correctly and always tried to be perfect.

The weeks following that declaration of love from Caleb were wonderful. They spent nearly every moment together. Oak Cottages were officially closed for winter; it was just Caleb and Sarah.

They ate when they were hungry, and made love when the mood struck, whether it was morning, afternoon or the middle of the night.

When he wrote, she painted.

The only dark cloud was that she hadn't spoken to her parents yet, she needed to phone them again. No, she decided she would write them a letter, without a return address. That way they couldn't condescend or intimidate her.

She grabbed some paper from the office, making sure it wasn't an Oak Cottages letterhead and started.

Dear Mother and Father

I hope this letter finds you in good health, as I am. I know you must be wondering when I am coming back and where I am, but I can tell you this, I am safe and I am happy.

I want to apologize to you for judging the way you live your life, it was wrong, but it was also wrong of you to expect me to follow in your footsteps, with no regard to what I wanted. I started painting again, I know you have never approved, but I won't stop again, not for anyone.

My paintings are selling in a local art gallery, and I must say they are selling quite well. I have also included a letter for Grant; I would appreciate it if you could make sure he receives it. I can't say exactly when I'll be back, but I hope we can put this behind us, and you can accept me for who I am and not who you want me to be. I'm sorry if this letter hurts you, mother. I know you never wanted me to paint and you wanted me to be married and settled.

I understand you wanted me sheltered, as I have been all these years, but the time has come for me to be who I am, make my own mistakes and live my life as I want.

Love Always
Your daughter, Sarah

As she put the letter aside, she decided to write Grant's letter too and grabbed another piece of paper from the desk.

Dear Grant

I know you must be mad and confused at me right now, but I hope you understand why I had to do it. I found out my father was having an affair. You can imagine my shock.

When I approached my mother to tell her, she knew. The whole situation just made me realize that we were going through with a wedding that we hadn't even planned. I couldn't do it.

You know I have always loved you, but we have never had passion.

You can try to deny it, but if you're honest you know it is true. We deserve more from life, Grant. We deserve passion, wild love and to decide who we marry ourselves. I hope you can see my decision wasn't taken lightly although with haste. I hope in time you can come to forgive me, and we can be the friends again we once were.

Love, Sarah.

Just as Sarah finished putting the completed letter in the envelope there was a knock on the door. It wouldn't be guests as there was a sign at the entrance indicating that Oak Cottages was closed for winter.

Cautiously she approached the back door. It was a thin middle aged man with crow's feet around his eyes, and he was puffing on a cigarette whilst looking at a notebook in his hand. He wore a fedora and a long brown coat.

She immediately recognized the face. It was her father's private investigator. Whenever her father had a case hanging in the balance, this man would show up late at night with information prudent to her father's current case.

Opening the door, she greeted him with apprehension, "Smitty."

"Sarah," he said solemnly.

"How'd you find me?" she enquired.

"Your phone call to you father." He stumped out the cigarette in a pot plant at the door. "I checked the phone records and traced the call to the phone booth in town." Still not connecting the dots, Sarah frowned. "It's a small town, Sarah. I only had to mention your name at the diner, and they told me exactly where I'd find you."

"Congratulations," Sarah said.

"Well, I'm in a bit of rush, our flight leaves in two hours, so if you'd get your things, we'd be on our way."

"I'm not going with you," Sarah stated.

"Oh yes you are, little lady, your father is paying me good money to bring you home, and I intend to cash in."

He caught her by the arm as Caleb walked in.

"Let her go." Caleb's voice was soft, but the tone of authority and malice caused Smitty to release her arm immediately.

"Smitty." Smitty held out his hand as if there were friendly introductions taking place. After realizing Caleb wasn't going to take it, he stuffed it back in his jacket pocket.

"What do you want?" Caleb asked, moving toward Sarah.

"Well, you see, I'm a friend of Sarah's father, and I've come to take her home," Smitty said jovially.

"I'm afraid she's not going anywhere unless she wants to." Caleb turned to Sarah and asked the rhetorical question, "Do you want to go with him?"

Sarah looked at Caleb, grateful he had come in; she would tell him that later. "No," she said definitively.

"Well then, seeing as she's not ready to leave, you can be on your way, Smitty." Caleb spat out his name.

"You see, sir, I would, but her father is paying quite a bit to collect her, so I'm afraid I can't leave without her."

"How much?"

"Excuse me, sir?"

"How much is Mr. Rothman paying you?" Caleb asked.

Smitty mentioned a large number; Caleb nodded his head as if he was talking about small change. Sarah tried to work out if she had that much, working the sum over and over in her head she realized she had just about enough left, but then she would have no money until Gladys came back. She was still thinking about the wedding dress she could sell to make up the funds, when Caleb spoke.

"Do you take checks?"

Smitty looked confused for a moment and then nodded.

"I'll give you five grand extra on condition you head to the airport and you don't bother Sarah again, and you can tell her parents to do the same."

Smitty smiled. "Well now, that's very kind of you, sir. I myself didn't want to drag her home kicking and screaming, I can see the little lady is happy."

"You can come with me for the check," Caleb said brusquely.

"Wait." Sarah grabbed the envelope and gave it to Smitty. "Could you make sure these letters are delivered?"

"Sure, sure, you have a nice time now." His eyes were dancing between Sarah and Caleb, indicating he knew they were sleeping together.

Caleb motioned for Smitty to follow, and, as they left, Sarah took a deep breath. It felt as if she had been holding her breath the entire time Caleb and Smitty were talking.

After dealing with Smitty and sending him on his way, Caleb found her in the kitchen, beating not kneading bread dough.

"What did the poor dough do to you?"

Sarah snickered, "Nothing, although I'm afraid I've beaten it to a pulp."

Caleb could tell she was still recovering from Smitty's visit, her shoulders were tense, and a deep frown had settled between her brows. "Are you alright?"

"Yes, I'm fine. I'll pay you back the money." She said it without looking at him.

"Sarah," and when she still didn't look up, he walked towards her and lifted her chin, "I didn't buy you." He wiped some flour that managed to find itself to her cheek away.

His words were simple, and exactly along the lines she had thought ever since Smitty had left.

Caleb gently stroked her cheek as he spoke, "I simply bought us time."

She nodded. She understood that, but still she didn't want to owe him anything.

Sensing this was a matter of pride, Caleb added, "Anyway do you know how much I made off my last book?"

Sarah shook her head from side to side.

"Let's just say if I *was* buying time, I could buy us a lifetime, and it would be worth every damn cent."

His hands settled on her shoulders as he pulled her closer for a kiss, and without thinking Sarah's hands moved to his face, finding her comfort in his kiss. A slow kiss that was meant to soothe soon turned to a furnace with flames of desire licking at edges.

Before they knew it they were both covered with flour and not minding at all.

Later that afternoon the phone rang in the study, just as Sarah was heading out to paint; she sprinted to answer it, thinking it was Gladys.

"Hello!" she greeted excitedly. She'd come to look forward to their little catch-ups.

"Sarah."

The somber tone, she instantly recognized as her father's voice.

"Father."

"You're on speaker, your mother and I would like a word with you."

"Alright," Sarah answered, resigned. "Hello, mother."

"Sarah," her mother answered.

"We received your letter," her father continued, "from Smitty. He tells me you are running a B&B?"

"No, I'm not running it, father, I'm simply taking care of it while the owner deals with a family crisis."

"And the man that paid Smitty off?" her father asked.

"His name is Caleb Sullivan." Sarah answered.

"I know his name, Sarah; he gave a check to a PI. Do you honestly not think that by now I don't know everything about him?"

"Then what about him, if you already know everything?" Sarah asked, irritated.

"Why did he pay Smitty off? Are you sleeping with him?"

Sarah didn't want to fight, but her father was taking things too far. "Yes, father, I am, and I am in love with him." Stopping before she said something hurtful, Sarah asked, "Did you read the letter?"

"Yes," Mr. Rothman answered matter-of-factly.

"And?" Sarah prompted.

"Your father and I feel that," Sarah's mother spoke for the first time since greeting Sarah, "since you feel so adamant about not wanting to be a part of our life, we are withdrawing all financial support until you come to your senses."

Sarah laughed. "Really? Have you checked my accounts? I haven't touched a dime since I left; I'm making my own way."

"More like sleeping with a man who pays your way, obviously," her mother replied harshly.

"He is not paying my way, he simply paid Smitty off. I'm making more than enough from my paintings and the work at Oak Cottages to support myself," Sarah fumed. "Now if you'll excuse me, let me go vacuum carpets and dabble with paints so I can continue doing just that."

With that final stab, Sarah banged the phone back on the hook.

Chapter 14

CALEB found Sarah late afternoon dueling a canvas with paintbrushes. She was at the front of the main house, reflecting the sun setting behind it. The main house was outlined in pencil; she was focused on the sunset surrounding it. With bold strokes she colored the canvas in hues of tangerine, dark cherry and plum. The strokes were definitive, hard and capturing the effect perfectly.

He had seen her paint before, but today was different. There was recklessness to her technique that made it more personal and more vibrant. This was her best work yet.

"Here you are," Caleb said as he approached. "I've been looking for you."

Sarah turned and nodded in acknowledgement before shifting back to focus on the painting.

"Is this your darker side?" Caleb asked jokingly. "If it is should I steer clear?"

"I don't know if it's my darker side," Sarah faced him brush in hand, "or if it's just me tired of fighting with my parents."

"You spoke to them?" Caleb moved forward.

"Obviously they phoned as soon as Smitty sent word of where I was ..." She let the words trail off.

"And?" Caleb prompted.

"And ... apparently I need to get back home, apparently I've had enough time playing," she fumed, "and apparently you're paying my way while I'm sleeping with you."

Caleb processed what she said and a frown settled on his forehead. "Sarah, that's ridiculous, you know it; I know it, so why let it bother you?"

Sarah put down her brush and wiped her hands on the cloth hanging from the easel. "That's what I've been trying to figure out." She sat on the grass and started plucking at the sprigs. "I think it's because my whole life I wanted their approval, I wanted them to be proud of me, and today I finally realized unless I don't do as I'm told, they never will be." A tear slipped down her cheek.

"Baby, it's their loss, not yours," Caleb said as he sat next to her and drew her into a hug. "If they can't accept you for who you are, it doesn't mean who you are isn't worth loving." He tilted her chin to look up at him. "It only means they tie conditions to their love, and that isn't love at all."

Sarah smiled at his kinds words, realizing they were true. She'd never been happier than during her time at Oak Cottages and she wasn't going to give up her happiness for her parents.

"I got one triumph, though," and she smiled at him through the tears. "They threatened to withdraw all their financial support, and I told them I don't need it, I've been selling my paintings." She gave a soft triumphant giggle. "I could actually hear my mother gasp from the other side of the room."

Caleb laughed. "I'm proud of you, and I don't mean that in a condescending way, I mean that in a respectful way." He brushed a strand of honey blonde hair behind her ear. "Not a lot of people have it in them to give up a life of luxury to follow their own dreams, and you did."

"You make me sound like a hero."

"You are," Caleb brushed her lips with his, "you're my hero."

Sarah smiled at his words and then attempted something she'd avoided doing for the past few weeks ever since he'd offered. "How's the book coming? Can I read it anytime soon?"

There was no anger in his eyes, just a peaceful determination. "Almost done, a few weeks at most."

That reality hit Sarah like a tidal wave; a few more weeks and he would leave.

Caleb comprehended the same time she did, and didn't want to think about leaving, so changed the subject swiftly. "Come, I want to show you something," He stood and helped her up.

"Where are we going?" Sarah asked as he pulled her along the narrow path.

"My cottage," Caleb said over his shoulder.

"Your cottage?" Sarah questioned.

Since Gladys left, Sarah had only been in to clean the cottage twice. Both times it was a mess. It seemed there was an explosion of paper surrounding his working space, clothes everywhere and it felt like she was intruding both times. He always came to her cottage; his had become more like his office the past few weeks.

As they reached the door, Caleb put his hands over her eyes. "Step carefully," he said as he guided her inside. Once inside he let his hand drop. "What do you think?"

Sarah looked around. Gone was the chaos and mess, it was tidy and the work space appeared organized. "Wow," she said as she glanced around again. "When did you do this?"

Caleb glanced around confused. "Oh, you mean clean it up?" He brushed his hands through his hair. "A few days ago. I'm busy with the FBI investigation, I need order for that," he said as if it made perfectly sense that he could write in chaos for weeks and then needed order for the final chapters. "That's not why you're here," he added excitedly, "so look around again."

Sarah did just that and found what he wanted to show her. Above the bed was one of her paintings. She remembered painting the Mount Desert Narrows the day after they made love for the first time. It was a calm scene, serene waters, shades of indigo and grey.

"Caleb, you didn't have to buy one of my paintings." She felt a little self-conscious.

"I didn't buy it because I know you, I bought it because it is beautiful ..." He paused and gave a mischievous grin. "... and because I saw you painting it the day after we made love for the first time."

Sarah smiled. "Thank you."

Caleb grinned back. "And now I can hang it in my house, and every time I look at it, or someone comments on it, I'll be reminded of you and that first night."

Sarah hugged him. They fit perfectly. Her head rested against his chest as his arms embraced her. She didn't know how she was going to let him go. He could be so abrasive and rude, and yet he had a beautiful and kind heart. She looked up at him, finding him deep in thought, as if he was playing with a thought in his mind.

"Something else on your mind?" she asked.

"Actually there is." He sounded serious.

"Well, let's have it?" Sarah prompted.

"It's my father's sixtieth birthday party this weekend, and I have to go."

"Of course you have to, I understand." Sarah smiled, "I'll be here when you get back."

"That's just it." Caleb chewed his cheek. "I don't want you to be here when I get back."

Sarah felt an ice pick stab through her heart. This was it.

It took all her courage to look him in the eye. "I understand," she said as she headed for the door.

Caleb swiftly caught up with her, and turned her to face him. "No, you don't," he smiled, "you really don't understand." He kissed her swiftly. "I'm fumbling here, badly; I haven't asked anyone to meet my parents since Elizabeth." He stumbled over the words as he started pacing.

"You want me to go with you?" Sarah asked incredulously.

He stopped and looked at her. "Yes, come with me to Wilmington, come meet my family."

"What about Oak Cottages?"

"They'll be fine for two nights; we'll phone Gladys and explain to her."

"Then she'll know."

Caleb grinned. "Then she'll know. Come on, say yes, Sarah."

Sarah chewed her bottom lip mulling the thought over in her mind. What better way to get a better picture of Caleb's life than meeting his family and seeing his home. "Yes, I'll go with you."

Chapter 15

THEY decided to fly to cut traveling time, not wanting to spend too long a period away from Oak Cottages. Sarah left the arrangements to Caleb as she prepared locking up Oak Cottages for three days and two nights.

Only when they reached the local airport did Sarah realize how wealthy Caleb was. They had a private charter standing by.

"Caleb?" Sarah asked as they were ushered into the plane.

"What?" he asked like a child caught stealing candy, a smile covering his face.

"A private charter," Sarah stated. "Really?"

Caleb shrugged. "There are no direct flights to Wilmington, we didn't want to drive sixteen hours, and I'm not zigzagging across the country if I can be there in two hours."

"You really did do well with your last book deal."

"Told you so," Caleb smiled.

The flight was short and uneventful, even if you weren't used to being served fresh cappuccinos and veal Carpaccio in flight. Sarah's father was wealthy, but she had never set foot in a charter plane before.

Caleb used the time to give Sarah a rundown of his family, to prepare her for the Sullivan onslaught waiting in Wilmington.

Sipping on a cappuccino, he began, "There's my father and my mother. They've been a unit since I can remember. They do mostly everything together. My father is a joker and likes almost everyone, but you don't cross him. The few people that have, never set foot in our house again."

Sarah raised her brows. "He sounds formidable."

"He is, but when its family there's nothing that can't be forgiven. He's a retired architect, although he still consults." Caleb smiled fondly before continuing, "Then there's my mother. We all know she's actually in charge of everyone and everything, but she lets my father believe he is. She's a free spirit that's never completely put her flowery past behind her. She's been involved in every charity you've heard of."

"Right, so we have an architect and a hippy?"

"More or less."

"Siblings?"

"I'm the eldest; I hope you know enough about me," Caleb winked. "And then there is Neal, barely a year younger than me. Neal permanently bears my darker side. It's not that he's unhappy, he's just very serious."

"What does *very serious* Neal do?"

"Prosecutor for Delaware State."

"Serious job." Sarah nodded.

"Next is Max, three years younger than Neal. Max and a friend started up a River Boating Company a few years back called 'Cape River Dreams'. He worked on a few charters during school, and liked the river so much he decided to make a life from it. He looks like a surfer, has my mom's free spirit, my father's sense of humor and a love for women."

"Sounds like an interesting guy, maybe I should go on a tour."

Caleb almost said 'not until there is a ring on your finger', and squashed the thought as soon as it popped into his mind. Max had always been popular with the girls; the thought that Sarah could be more interested in him scared him a little.

"We won't have time," he teased.

Sarah quickly understood the jealousy underneath the teasing and felt a warm tingle. "Right, so tell me about your sister."

"Lisa." Caleb frowned and scratched his chin with the hand not holding his cappuccino. "Lisa is still studying but living at home. She's studying to become a marine biologist."

"Brains check." Sarah made a tick mark in the air.

"That she's got, and an undiluted belief in happy ever afters."

"Well, there's nothing wrong with that."

"I suppose not, it's just not fun mopping up the tears after the break-ups."

They talked a bit more about his siblings, and how he got along with them. Sarah was a little intimidated, but she couldn't wait to meet the Sullivans.

They landed in Wilmington late afternoon.

Sarah couldn't help but tease, "I trust there is a limousine waiting outside?"

Caleb laughed. "No, only Max."

As they reached the arrivals area, Caleb wheeling their luggage on a trolley, a shout immersed from the crowd, "There he is, my brother the bookworm."

Sarah's gaze settled on a muscled, blonde Adonis with piercing blue eyes. His hair was ruffled and his smile easy. The brothers didn't look related at all.

As he approached, Caleb stepped away from the trolley and grabbed Max in a bear hug. "Miss me, blondy?"

Sarah watched the exchange, as they bantered and hugged easily. Here was only love and respect, and a bond forged from growing up side by side. Sarah had always regretted being an only child, and seeing them together only made the regret more intense.

"Max, I'd like you to meet someone." Caleb indicated for Sarah to come forward. "Sarah Rothman, meet Max Sullivan."

Sarah shook hands with the blonde Adonis, and still couldn't find any resemblance.

Picking up on her curiosity, Max said, "Don't worry, nobody else believes it either. I've always said Caleb was a stray my parents picked up."

Sarah laughed, and Caleb clarified, "I take after my father's side, and goldilocks here takes after my mother."

"Pleased to meet you, Max," Sarah said when the laughter subsided.

They walked to the car and after Caleb placed the luggage in the trunk he held out his hand, indicating to Max to pass him the keys.

"Come on, man," Max complained, "I promise I'll stay on my side of the road and keep to the speed limit."

Caleb laughed. "That's the best joke I've heard in a long time."

He eventually maneuvered the keys from Max and efficiently drew away from the curb. They drove toward Wrightsville beach; that was all Sarah could make out from the roads they were taking.

After a short while, Caleb drew up to a one story house with beach access. The house looked inviting. It was white with grey shutters, and a lot of windows. Caleb got out and started unloading the luggage. As soon as their entire luggage was in the driveway, he tossed the keys to Max. "See you tonight."

Max saluted them before getting onto the car and reversing out of the driveway. When he screeched away, Sarah realized why Caleb didn't want Max to drive.

Caleb took her hand and indicated at the house. "Mi casa, Su casa."

"This is your house?" Sarah asked. "I just thought we were going directly to your parents."

"I thought we'd make a short detour and pick up my car first." He grabbed the bags and headed for the front door.

As soon as they were inside Sarah could tell it was a bachelor's place. There was minimal furniture and what that was there appeared well lived in and comfortable.

The whole house had a glass fronted view of the ocean. The appliances were top of the range and the LED screen mounted on the far wall made going to the cinema completely redundant.

Caleb disappeared into a hallway as she walked towards the windows. The view was amazing. Miles and miles of ocean. She couldn't imagine why he would need to go anywhere else to write.

His hands settled around her waist. "Like it?" he whispered close to her ear.

She leaned into his mouth, and obligingly he kissed her. "It's beautiful, Caleb; I don't understand why you don't write here, although I'm not complaining, otherwise I wouldn't have met you."

"I don't write here because everyone knows I'm here, my agent, publicist, family, friends, and the interruptions always end up in arguments," he laughed. "As you know, I don't take the interruptions well."

Sarah chuckled, "I understand completely." She turned towards him. "Is there time for me to grab a quick shower before we go to your parents"?"

"Only if I'm invited."

Caleb smiled as he put his mouth against hers and started backing her towards the bedroom. He began peeling her clothes off, without ever letting his lips leave hers. He thought that by now this burning hunger would've been sated, but whenever he touched her, it was there. Intoxicating. Overwhelming. Primal desire that caused his heart to become heavy with love.

He took his time showing her.

Chapter 16

THE shower wasn't quick; it was slow, intoxicatingly slow and wonderful. Sarah felt refreshed and revitalized, and it had nothing to do with the shower. As she dressed in a pair of jeans she suddenly felt awkward - this wasn't she wanted to wear when she met Caleb's parents.

Her mother's voice hummed in her mind, *Sarah, you simply don't wear jeans anywhere but in the privacy of your room.* As she buttoned up the white cotton shirt, Caleb walked in.

"You look fresh as a daisy."

Sarah looked at him. "I don't feel comfortable; what are your parents going think of me arriving for dinner in jeans? It's completely inappropriate."

Caleb roared with laughter. "Sarah, you've never sounded more the southern bell than you do right now." He gave her a smack on the bum. "Besides, will it make you feel any better if I guarantee you my mother will be wearing jeans?"

Sarah's eyes widened. "You can't be serious?"

"Would you think any less of her?"

"No, of course not, it just my mother always deemed jeans inappropriate attire," she shrugged.

"Well, I deem your mother's opinions inappropriate." He moved toward her. "Jeans are never inappropriate, especially not on you." He looked her up and down, and Sarah felt his gaze heat her skin.

"If you really think it's alright, I'm ready to leave." She grabbed her tote bag from a chair in the corner before they got delayed, again.

It took about twenty minutes to arrive at Caleb's parent's home in a quiet suburban part of Wilmington. The house was a Victorian two story, with a wraparound porch.

It was a moss green with white trim and a tire hung on a rope from a tree in the front yard. As they parked in the driveway that ran adjacent to the house, Sarah noticed the swing on the porch.

Caleb came around to open the door for her.

"This is a lovely home," Sarah commented as they rounded the house to the back door.

Caleb shrugged. "We've been here forever."

As they rounded the car a man approached from the garage.

"Well, I'll be ... Caleb?"

He was nearing sixty, presumably Caleb's father. He was balding and his hair was turning grey, but Sarah could see that it was once the ink black color Caleb had. He had the same green eyes. As he walked towards them, smile in place, the crow's feet at the corner of his eyes deepened. Sarah could see this was a man who enjoyed laughing.

"Hi, Dad." Caleb walked forward and gripped his dad in a bear hug.

For the second time that day Sarah saw two grown men hugging, back home it was always polite handshakes. Obviously this family was comfortable with public displays of affection.

He slapped Caleb on the back a few times and drew back. "You didn't even let us know you were coming."

"Thought I'd surprise you, that is what you wanted for your birthday, right?"

"Of course. Now where are your manners, introduce me to your young lady." He came towards Sarah with an inviting smile. Sarah liked how he called her Caleb's 'young lady'.

"Mackenzie Sullivan, meet Sarah Rothman," Caleb introduced and then turned toward Sarah. "Sarah, this is my dad." He said it with a proud smile.

"Pleased to make your acquaintance," Sarah said with the acquired grace of a southern debutante.

Caleb's father shot Caleb a questioning look at the formal greeting, but recovered before Sarah could notice. "Please call me Mac, everyone else does." Mac smiled at her.

"Alright," Sarah smiled back.

Mac's arm came around her shoulders. "Well, come on in, Sarah. Susan will have me skinned for keeping you out here to myself."

They walked into the kitchen to the lovely scent of beef stew.

"Suzie, look what just rolled up." Mac ushered Caleb and Sarah forward.

"Caleb!" She nearly shouted the greeting whilst wiped her hands on an apron protecting her jeans.

Sarah smiled, thinking of Caleb's guarantee of jeans earlier. Caleb's mother wore a t-shirt with Hawaiian floral print. Her hair was blonde, just reaching her shoulders with a natural wave to it. She recognized the same ice blue eyes she saw when meeting Max. Her waist apron boasting the words *EAT ME* indicated she had a sense of humor.

Before Caleb could greet his mom properly or turn to introduce Sarah, Susan swiftly took Sarah's hands. "Welcome, dear, I'm Susan."

The hands holding hers were soft, strong and reassuring; all the fear of meeting Caleb's parents vanished. "Thank you, I'm Sarah Rothman."

She pulled Sarah in for a comfortable hug. Sarah couldn't help but hug back and smell the light flowery scent Susan was wearing.

When they both pulled back, Caleb piped up morosely, "Hi, mom, great to see you too."

"Oh, you big baby, I missed you too!" Susan said as she hugged Caleb. She was short and her head barely made his chest.

Sarah smiled at this tall tough man hugging this older woman so tightly; this was what parental love should be like, Sarah couldn't help but think.

"We thought we'd surprise you for dad's shindig," Caleb said as he grabbed a chair at the kitchen table, "that's if you can make room for two more."

Susan swatted him with a dishcloth. "Don't be absurd, you know I don't cater for late arrivals," she said with a scowl before laughingly turning to Sarah. "Of course you're welcome, dear."

Sarah now understood where the easy banter and comfortable interaction that she witnessed earlier between Max and Caleb came from.

"Is Lisa home yet?" Caleb asked, looking towards the hallway leading from the kitchen.

Susan moved back to the stove. "No, she'll be in shortly; she quickly went to get me some potatoes."

Caleb nodded. "You might want to add some more beef as well, Max is also coming tonight."

Susan beamed back at him. "Yes, he sent me a text."

"Sarah, you're not vegetarian, are you?" Mac asked Sarah jokingly. "We're big on casseroles around here."

"Actually ..." Sarah couldn't help but tease back, her expression apologetic. At the worried look that passed between Mac and Susan, she quickly added, "Oh no, not at all, that stew smells wonderful."

A roar of laughter exploded in the kitchen.

Caleb was relieved Sarah was feeling comfortable enough to joke with his father. "Mom, you should really try and wrangle Sarah's fried chicken recipe from her, it'll be worth the struggle," he suggested while winking at Sarah.

"Honestly, Caleb, it's not *that* great." Sarah said.

"Not that good?" Caleb stated incredulously. "I ate seven pieces, SEVEN!"

"Caleb has never been a big eater, so that's saying something. Sarah, it would be lovely if you could share it with me, my fried chicken never completely hits the spot, but I don't suppose you brought your recipe book along?" Susan looked at Sarah with a raised eyebrow.

"I know it by heart," Sarah conceded, "and I'd be glad to write it down for you." Sarah looked around the kitchen, and saw there were onions peeled, but they still needed to be chopped, a bowl of beans that still needed to be prepared. "Susan, would you mind if I help you?"

Sarah didn't want to sit watching the woman go through all this trouble because of their impromptu visit.

"That would be lovely, dear." Susan took the chopping block and a knife, and set them in front of Sarah with the onions. "Don't tear up now," Susan said, indicating the onions and turned back towards the stove.

The statement itself, in its simplicity, nearly had Sarah tearing up. She had never felt so welcomed and so accepted, not even in her own home. Sarah started chopping the onions efficiently and when she sniffed, Mac and Susan laughed, commenting on the onion-emotions; only Caleb understood and winked at her supportively. He knew he could always count on his mother to make anyone feel welcome in their home.

They were all seated at dinner and Sarah was overwhelmed with the congeniality of it. Lisa had blown in like a fresh spring breeze talking about mollusks and whales, wearing a long flowery print skirt and a colorful cardigan, and although she had her father's black eyes, she had her mother's free spirit.

Max arrived talking about the tour he just finished and teasing Caleb to invite Sarah for a private tour. She wouldn't be meeting Neal tonight, but she thought it was for the best. Sarah tried to follow the conversation; between them catching up with Caleb, they were all speaking simultaneously and throwing in stories about Caleb's childhood for her benefit.

The Sullivans' didn't realize how precious it was what they had in this dining room. The unity, the understanding, the acceptance. Even though their personalities were different, they all had the same good sense of humor.

Mac was truly interested in his children and their pursuits, and listened when they told him about their day.

Chattering on about a rare mussel, Susan and Lisa walked in with the casserole dish and the rice.

"Dig in!" Susan exclaimed as she set the dish down in the center of the table. In a practiced routine, plates were passed around, loaded and passed back.

"This smells delicious, Susan," Sarah said.

"Mom's food is the best," Max said between bites. "I've always said if I can find a woman that cooks better than my mother, I'll marry her first chance I get."

"That's means you have to actually date them long enough for them to cook for you, moron," Lisa teased.

"It will also mean you need more in your kitchen than a microwave and freezer," Caleb said, waving with his fork.

"She needs to be something worth looking at as well!" Mac said with a booming voice. "You kids know nothing about love; it's all in the cooking and in their eyes." When he had Susan's attention he said, "If you're going to be looking into your children's eyes for the rest of your life, you need to make sure they're something to look at."

Everyone laughed, including Sarah. Susan gave him a light shove, before he caught her in a hug and mumbled something into her hair that had her blushing and laughing.

"So, Sarah, Caleb said you're from Savannah?" Susan asked, trying to change the subject, a glow still warming her cheeks.

"That's right, southern born and bred." Sarah smiled and focused on her food, hoping no one else will ask something about why she left.

"You met in Maine at Oak Cottages?" Lisa raised her eyebrows in question.

"That's right, yes; I'm helping the owner out for a while."

"Why did you leave the South and head up North?" Max asked, lying back in his chair.

Sarah didn't miss a beat; she knew the question was coming. "I wanted to explore a bit and I had time."

"Sarah's an artist," Caleb said before Max could ask any more questions.

"Really?" Mac asked. "What do you do?"

Sarah laughed, giddy at the thought of being introduced as an artist for the first time. "I paint."

"Oh, wonderful, we've been meaning to have a portrait done of the family."

"Not people, mom," Caleb corrected, "landscapes, fruit, flowers, stuff like that."

"Oh, I'd love to see some of your work," Susan said excitedly.

"Well, I'm still quite new at it, I only started selling recently," Sarah said shyly.

"All the more reason to show me; if you're any good, and I'm sure you are, I have a lot of friends who love a great landscape." She winked at Sarah.

The back door slammed shut.

Mac immediately stood up, and said in a serious tone, "That must be Neal." As Mac headed towards the kitchen, conversation resumed around the table.

After a while Mac returned with a tall blonde man following him. He had a boxer's build and blue eyes. She could immediately see this was Neal from the family resemblance to Max.

He was slightly older, and whereas Max's unkempt blonde hair was tinged with highlights from hours in the sun, Neal's was a darker blond and cropped short.

"Sarah, this is Neal."

Neal nodded in her direction, but she could see he was distracted. "Pleased to meet you, Neal," Sarah said and focused on her plate.

"You too, hey everybody."

Greetings went around the table, and Susan finally settled Neal in with a plate and a glass of wine.

"So what happened today?" Mac asked with that serious tone.

"What do you mean what happened?" Neal bit back.

"You weren't due to come by tonight, although we never mind that you do. But you always come by looking like that when something bad happened in court," Mac said.

Everyone else was quiet waiting for Neal's response.

"I don't want to talk about it," came the brisk reply.

"Honey, if you're not going to talk to your family about it, who are you going to talk to?" Susan said as she placed her hand on his arm.

"Do we need to beat up someone for you?" Caleb asked.

Neal wiped his mouth with his napkin, knowing that they wouldn't stop until he told them. "A rapist walked today." He took a big slug of wine. "Because a stupid nurse labeled the rape kit date incorrectly."

"Oh, Neal," Susan said kindly, "I'm sure you did all you could."

"You can't win 'em all, son, you knew that going in," Mac said in support.

"I know, I just hate to see them walking free."

Conversation turned away from Neal's case and toward gardening. When all the plates were empty Sarah offered to take them to the kitchen. Voices around the table chorused complaint, but Sarah could make out the gist of it, that they didn't expect her to do it.

"I really don't mind and, after all, you've been such great hosts it's the least I can do." As Sarah set the plates down next to the sink, she heard someone behind her. It was Susan. "Dinner was really wonderful," Sarah smiled.

"Indeed it was." Susan contemplated on what she wanted to say.

Sensing she had something on her mind, Sarah waited patiently.

"You know you're the first woman Caleb's brought home ever since we lost Elizabeth. I take it he's told you about her?"

Understanding the gravity of the statement, Sarah nodded. "He has. He blames himself."

"I know, but bringing you home to meet us, mean he is putting some of what happened in the past."

"I've enjoyed meeting you all."

"I haven't seen Caleb smile or look as happy in a long time as he did tonight. Thank you for bringing him back to life."

Not knowing how to respond, Sarah simply nodded. Susan stepped toward her and gave her a hug that nearly had Sarah in tears again. She could get used to being hugged all the time.

"Your family is wonderful," Sarah said as they reversed out of the driveway later that evening.

"Thanks, although we can be a meddling, teasing bunch, underneath it all we love each other."

"You're all so different, and your parents seem to embrace it."

"They do," Caleb said, glancing at Sarah. "What's on your mind?"

"Oh, not much," Sarah said, gazing out the window. "I just never thought families could be like that, all loving and teasing at the same time. My parents were always judging and demanding, nothing like yours. I can't ever remember my father even telling a joke, and with yours it comes naturally."

"Well, you can share mine," he said without thinking.

Sarah looked at him quickly, realizing he didn't think before he said it. She laughed. "Don't look so shocked, I'm not planning on dragging you to the altar because I like your parents."

"Who said you'll be the one doing the dragging?" Caleb said, raising one cocky eyebrow.

Chapter 17

MAC'S party was a backyard barbecue despite the autumn chill. The whole yard was decorated with triangular flags, and tables and umbrellas were set up, along with towering mobile gas heaters.

Four barbecues perfumed the air with the scents of beef grilling. It was a chilly day but no one seemed to notice the weather. Champagne flowed as freely as the Mississippi, and the many faces started to blend for Sarah.

Not knowing anyone, she had stayed at Caleb's side. She was nursing her second glass of champagne at a table near the kitchen, when Caleb went to check on the barbecue. She didn't mind being on her own for a bit, she enjoyed watching.

Observing the different types of people, how some of them chatted with exaggeration, explaining with their hands, Sarah could almost make out the entire conversation from watching those gestures. Others would gossip, as people do at these events, and

Sarah spotted them too, heads close, with a quick scan of the nearby area before launching into a story.

Caleb had earlier introduced her to Elizabeth's parents and her sister Megan. From meeting them Sarah could tell they cared a lot for Caleb and didn't blame him for their daughter's accident.

She took another sip of champagne when Megan came and sat down beside her. Megan pounced, "He doesn't love you, you know."

Sarah nearly sputtered champagne all over the table. "Excuse me?"

"Caleb, he doesn't love you. He doesn't look at you the way he used to look at my sister."

Not knowing how to respond to such an inappropriate comment, Sarah opted for higher ground. "I'm sorry about the loss of your sister."

"Yes, you should be. You're sleeping with the man that caused it!" Megan's eyes were burning with rage and contempt.

"Excuse me; I need to visit the ladies room." Sarah stood up and turned to leave, scanning the crowd for Caleb.

As she spotted him at the other end of the yard talking to Max over a barbecue, a hand caught her arm in a vice grip. Megan was very thin, and Sarah couldn't believe the grip she had. She tried to wrench her arm away, but Megan's nails bit into her skin.

"It's not fair!" Megan hissed at her. "He killed Elizabeth and now he's pretending like she never existed."

"Of course she existed," Sarah answered, not wanting to cause a scene. "He told me about her, he loved her very much."

"If he did he wouldn't have let her die." A tear slipped down Megan's cheek.

"I'm sorry."

"Does he bring you flowers? Does he tell you he loves you?" Megan gauged the shock on Sarah's face as a cue that she was hitting a sore spot. "Caleb should've died, not my sister. I hope *you* die!"

"Is there a problem here?" Neal's voice from behind Sarah had both ladies turning toward him startled. Neal noticed the white knuckled grip Megan had on Sarah. He briskly pulled it off Sarah's arm, and in the struggle a nail tore skin and fierce flames ignited from exposed nerves.

"It's not fair!" Megan shouted as Neal drew Sarah towards the house. "He'll never love you!"

Neal walked her straight to the kitchen sink and started running water over the scratches. "Are you okay?"

Sarah shook her head; she was confused - what had just happened? She needed to get away. "I need to go." She pulled her arm from Neal.

"You don't, but I understand if you want to leave." He put his hands on her shoulders. "What just happened wasn't your fault, I heard it all."

"You heard?"

"Yes, all of it. I always thought that girl was nuts, but I didn't realize it was that bad."

"Caleb said she had a breakdown at the funeral."

"Yes, it was horrible. But apparently she's stable now." A look passed between them and they both laughed.

Sarah put her hand over the scratches trying to appease the burn.

"You need to know what she said isn't true. I can't say that he loves you, but I can tell you he's never looked at someone the way he looks at you since Elizabeth passed."

Sarah nodded, dumbfounded.

"Wait here, I'll get Caleb to take you home."

Within seconds Caleb was in the kitchen holding her. "What the hell happened? Neal said he had to save you from Megan."

"I'll tell you about it later, right now I just want to leave."

Caleb grabbed his keys from the counter. "Come on."

"I have to thank your parents." Sarah said as she was pulled towards the car.

"You can thank them over the phone."

The drive back to Wrightsville beach was quiet; you could cut the tension in the car with a blunt knife.

Sarah was rattled from her encounter with Megan. From what Neal said, she understood with her mind that Megan was unstable, but her heart struggled to let go of the fear that what Megan said was true. That she could never replace Elizabeth.

She didn't want to. But no woman wanted to live in the shadow of another.

When they reached Caleb's house, Sarah had reached the conclusion that what they had between them would need to come to an end. Sooner rather than later. Before it hurt too much.

"Are you alright?" Caleb asked later as he emerged from the shower. Sarah was already in bed. He didn't know what Megan had said to her, but Sarah had been quiet since. She was pulling away from him.

She didn't feel like talking, or rehashing the attack from Megan. Instead she went to him and framed his face with her hands. The steam was still coming off his back and a trail of drops ran from his hair down the front of his chest. She moved in closer and could feel his breath on her lips.

Cobalt blue eyes met grass green, and the anticipation of what was about to happen hung between them. Sarah drew out the moment, wanting to extend every part of their love making, for soon she would need to leave him. She softly rubbed her lips over his.

"How is it that every time you touch me, my whole body ignites, Sarah?"

"It's a good thing I've come to like playing with fire." She slid her hands down to pull the towel away from his waist.

Caleb framed her face with his hands, brushing his thumbs over her cheeks. The ache that started in his chest a few weeks ago was now warmed with love. He wanted to show her. He needed her to know what she meant to him. He slowly led her to the bed, his eyes not leaving hers for a moment. The sound of the surf breaking against the sand floated through the open windows. He stood and lit a few candles he placed strategically around the room earlier that day.

Sarah sat on the bed watching him. Her heart beat to an age old rhythm when Caleb prowled towards her. Sinking into the soft bedcover, he sat down next to her and slowly started pulling her shirt over her head.

"You're skin is like alabaster in the candlelight, Sarah."

Sarah looked away shyly; Caleb took her chin and gently turned her to face him. "You are beautiful, and I need you to listen when I tell you that. Do you hear me?"

Sarah nodded and met his gaze head on.

Caleb lowered his head and met her lips with a probing tongue; soon they tasted and explored each other, blazing desire meeting soft strokes. Teetering on the edge of a cliff, before they knew it, they tripped over and fell in love.

When their flight landed back in Maine the following day, Sarah was relieved to be home. She was surprised that she had started thinking of Maine as home.

She had glossed over the conversation with Megan after they made love last night. She didn't want him to know the full weight of the blame that Megan harbored.

She also didn't want to explore exactly what Megan said about Caleb not loving her the way he loved Elizabeth. Only Neal knew exactly what was said, and though Megan was a bit unstable, the whole incident had left her shaken.

Caleb had made it even harder when he handed her the first pages of his manuscript to read on the plane on the way home. Reading about anger and enjoyment a psychopath derived from hurting young girls, Sarah now understood why Caleb found himself in a dark place while writing. She couldn't help but fall for him a little more.

She tried to ignore the feelings she had for Caleb. They were just having fun while they were in Maine.

Nothing had been discussed about futures or pursuing their relationship once they left Oak Cottages, but in her heart she knew she loved Caleb.

She would never tell him that.

This was something she'd work through on her own. Just like the situation with her parents. She hadn't heard from them since their last conversation, but when they reached Oak Cottages a letter had arrived addressed to her. She recognized the handwriting as her mother's and tore it open immediately.

Dear Sarah

We trust you are still hesitant to take on your responsibilities as a Rothman and choose to live as a beholden chambermaid. If you do not come home and rectify this situation before the New Year, you will leave us no choice but to change our will.

Yours Sincerely
Mother

Sarah crumpled the piece of paper and threw it in the bin, just as Caleb walked in.

"Bad news?"

"Letter from my parents."

"What did it say?

"Come home, fix your mistakes or we'll disown you, that's about it."

"You can't be serious."

"Oh, I am, and you know the worst part of it is, they still don't get it. They honestly think their money matters to me."

"Oh baby, I wish I could fix this for you." Caleb drew her closer and nudged her head under his chin. Sarah leaned into the warmth and the comfort she found there and said on a sigh, "It's not yours to fix."

Chapter 18

SARAH spent the next few days painting, cleaning the cottages, and doing just anything to keep her busy. Gladys would be returning next week and Sarah didn't want to leave her with a backlog when she left.

Visiting Wilmington had made her realize how she really felt about Caleb. It wasn't just fun anymore. She was developing deep feelings, deeper than she thought possible. The way her heart skipped when he smiled at her. The way she couldn't help but smile when he ate potato chips in bed, or the way he always sang in the shower.

She couldn't avoid or ignore the passion that heated her whole body when he kissed her. She was going to get hurt. She was trying to put a little distance between them. She didn't want to live in the shadow of Elizabeth and the love they had.

It was hard, harder than walking out on her wedding. Last

night she had claimed a headache and told Caleb he could work instead of keep her company; his book was nearing the end and he didn't want to lose momentum, so he went to work in his cottage.

Sarah couldn't fall asleep without the weight of his arm over her; she woke up in the middle of the night turning to make sleep-hazed love to him, to find the sheets next to her cool. She was starting to look for him everywhere, wanting to tell him everything.

It was time for them to end whatever this was. She didn't say any of it to Caleb; she decided she would tell him next week … before she went home. Once Gladys was back it was time to face her parents.

The following morning she had her purse in hand, and a list of supplies to collect and errands to run. When she reached her car, she couldn't believe what she was seeing.

All four of her tires were slashed.

Immediately she thought of her father, and the ends he would pursue to achieve his goal or to make a point. This had Attorney Rothman written all over it. Furious with her father, she stalked to Caleb's cabin and after a brisk knock walked in.

"I need to borrow your car," she all but shouted at him.

"Okay, want to tell me why?" He went to the counter and handed her the keys.

"My father had my tires slashed." She grabbed the keys and walked towards the door.

"Your father did what?" Caleb followed her to the parking lot.

"This is exactly the type of thing my father would do." Sarah opened Caleb's passenger door and dumped her purse and list on the seat, slamming the door shut. "An attorney with his win record doesn't always win by playing clean. And they always have people on payroll willing to help the game along."

"You mean you think your father would have your tires slashed because you walked out on your wedding?"

"No, I'm telling you my father would do this to teach me a lesson. To tell me I won't be able to manage on my own. So now he's throwing some spanners in the works of my new life, hoping I'll run back home."

"Is that what you are going to do?"

"And give him the satisfaction that he won? Not a chance. I'm not even going to phone him."

"Want me to fix it?"

Sarah cobalt blue eyes whipped towards his spitting ice. "I do not want you to fix it or to pay to have it fixed. I'll get a mechanic in town to come and fix it."

Caleb held up his hands. "I promise I won't fix it. See you later."

Sarah found a mechanic in town, Lila's fiancé, Mitch. He was eager to help, although he only managed to get to Oak Cottages late afternoon. When he was finished, he passed Sarah the bill. After giving her a hefty discount, it still ate up a large chunk of the money she had left from the sale of her car.

She would need to sell some more paintings to tide her over; luckily when Gladys came back she would pay her for her time as was agreed.

As she walked to her cottage after seeing off Mitch, she felt as if someone was watching her. She turned around and scanned the bushes, but found no sign of movement. To no one in particular she flipped a bird in the direction of the bushes. If her father had a lackey watching her, at least he would have seen it.

She let herself into her cottage and sat on the couch catching her breath and willing her temper to cool. She couldn't believe her father would go this far. It was ridiculous. She wouldn't call him on it, instead she'd let him seethe and wonder if the job was carried out. That would serve him right.

When Caleb opened the door she nearly jumped out of her skin.

"Careful there," Caleb smiled. He could see she was rattled. He couldn't conceive how a parent would go to these lengths to manipulate a child. Maybe it was time he phoned the infamous Mr. Rothman.

Sarah tried to quiet the shivers that were running through her body. She was letting her father win if she was going to jump at every little noise or sound.

"Your keys are on the counter, thanks."

"Did you manage to get it fixed?" Caleb asked as he sat down next to her.

"Yes, a mechanic in town came out and replaced all four tires. He said they had a couple of teenagers some years back doing this in town, but it was always just one tire and never this far out." She shook her head. "He agrees this wasn't just some errant teenagers."

Knowing Sarah needed to get her mind off what happened, he suggested, "How about I cook tonight and you drink some wine?"

"You cook?"

"Well, I can't cook like you do, but toasted cheese is widely known as food."

Sarah laughed for the first time since that morning. "Yes, they are part of a special food group called junk food."

"Well then, junk food and wine it is."

Sarah found herself sitting at the kitchen island drinking expensive Shiraz while Caleb cut inch thick slices of cheese and placing it on the bread. She felt the fear and anger slide away like mist before the sun.

"There is a flat plate sandwich toaster in the pantry."

"Excuse me, what did you just say?" Caleb tossed a dishcloth at her. "Even I have my standards. True toasted cheese is made in a pan. Hot pan, little oil, a flat plate sandwich toaster will never be able to achieve that kind of perfection."

He was right. Sarah had never eaten toasted cheese sandwiches that were made in a pan, but there was a difference. A big enough difference so that the toasted cheese actually complemented the expensive Shiraz.

She would miss this when she left next week.

The easy conversation, the way Caleb could make her laugh. She would even miss his miserable moods when talk was overrated and he simply needed to be held.

She couldn't help but wonder if it was like this between him and Elizabeth before she passed.

Were they also this comfortable with each other? She didn't want to think of their relationship, but Megan's words kept haunting her. Haunting her just enough to let doubt slide in through the small cracks in her confidence.

Sensing something was bothering her, Caleb intruded into her thoughts. "Want to tell me what's troubling you?"

Knowing she couldn't ask him about Elizabeth, afraid of the answer, she improvised, "Thinking about my car."

"Yeah, I could imagine that's bothering you. Still not going to phone your father?"

"No, he wants me to run to daddy and cry and ask for money," Sarah wiped the cheese oil from her hands with a napkin. "I won't be doing that."

"I get it, I completely do, but why would he go these lengths?"

"Caleb, my parents have never seen having me as a blessing," she answered with a sigh. "My conception was planned, and every stage of growing up was mapped out in detail, even which classes to attend at what age. I think they became so consumed with having the perfect child; they never stopped to consider what I wanted. And before I found out he was cheating, that was fine with me." She ran her hands through her hair. "I had a good life, until my eyes opened and I realized they would never accept me for who I am."

Caleb walked over to her and started rubbing the tension from her shoulders.

"I had to get away to realize who I am, and now that I have, I won't be able to go back to being the perfectly manipulated debutante."

"So don't go back," Caleb said as his fingers worked magic on the tension in her neck.

"You and I know I have to. I have to try to make them accept me or …"

"Or?" Caleb started working his fingers into the back of her hair, running up and down her scalp.

"Or they can't be part of my life anymore." Sarah turned to look at him.

She wished she could push this doubt about him far from her mind. Wished she could forget what Megan had said. Everything was wonderful before going to Wilmington. She was starting to regret she had ever agreed to go. Besides the attack from Megan, she had realized how much she had missed by not having parents who cared about what she wanted.

Caleb leaned in to whisper a soft kiss over her ear. Sarah leaned into him and turned her head so she could meet his lips with her own.

His eyes were watching her in the soft lighting; she could smell the wine and the essence that was him. That slow velvet desire intoxicated her. It pushed its way down to her core where she could feel heat start to build. As Caleb slowly started nibbling her bottom lip, she couldn't help the breath that hitched from her mouth.

He ran his hands softly over her arms and turned the chair, they were face to face, Sarah sitting on the kitchen stool, Caleb standing between her legs. He leaned in to kiss her slowly, running his hands up her thighs.

Sarah couldn't stand it anymore. She wanted him. She wanted him inside her. She wanted to forget today, forget Megan, forget Elizabeth, and just be with the man she loved. Next week all of this would change.

She tugged his shirt from his jeans and ran her hands up his chest. His torso was warm and lean; she could feel the muscles tremble as she grazed them with her fingertips.

When she started running her fingers down and fiddled with his belt, Caleb took her hands in his.

"I think we need to take this somewhere more private."

Sarah knew what he meant, they had made love in the kitchen before, but the strokes, the touches, and the kisses of tonight were meant for slow seduction, a bed would be better. Not wanting to let her head takeover, Sarah took his hands and led him up the stairs to the bedroom where she spent her first night at Oak Cottages. She closed the door behind him, and slowly slipped out of her shoes, keeping her eyes on his the whole time.

"Sarah, you're killing me. I never thought watching a woman remove her shoes could be sexy, but I'm damn near begging."

Sarah gave a low husky laugh and kept looking straight at him as she undid the zipper on her jean and started wiggling it down to her ankles. She stepped out of them and lifted the hem of her shirt, and pulled it achingly slow over her head.

She was standing before him in only her underwear. The seduction of lace hinted at what was underneath.

Caleb ran a hand over his face before he let out his breath and moved toward her.

"No," Sarah said as she reached behind her back, "tonight I'm seducing you ..." She flicked the clip of the bra and it slid to the floor soundlessly.

Watching the hunger and need in his eyes build, was a type of power Sarah had never known. She reveled in the power. She cherished the way he looked at her. She slid her thumbs into the hips of her panty and slowly pulled it down until she was standing in front of him wearing nothing but a smile.

"You're not allowed to touch or taste until I say so."

Sarah walked towards Caleb and tugged the hem of his shirt over his shoulders to reveal his muscled shoulders.

Caleb was all but panting. As she slid her hands in the front of his waistband to undo the buttons on his jean he had to hold his breath to keep from grabbing her and throwing her on the bed.

Sarah slowly slid his jeans to the floor, his jockey following. They were standing watching each other, Sarah enjoying the power, Caleb waiting for permission to devour her.

She didn't need to say a word. She simply took his hand and smiled. Caleb allowed the need, the hunger and his desire to take over.

Chapter 19

THE light teased Sarah awake, and she reached beside her to feel for Caleb, but found the bed empty. She was glad for that. It gave her a minute to compose herself. Last night was the most wonderful night in her life.

There was a difference between making love and making love with someone you loved. It made her vulnerable, giving him everything along with her heart, and she wanted to believe he felt the same way. Neither of them dared to admit to their feelings for each other.

Sarah smiled to herself as she dressed. She would always have this. She would always have her time with Caleb to use as a yardstick in ensuing relationships. She doubted any one of them could come close to theirs, but at least she knew what it felt like to love someone.

She entered the kitchen, coffee aromas thick in the air, and saw there was a police officer sitting at the table with Caleb.

"What's going on?" Sarah demanded.

Caleb stood to pour her some coffee. "Our cottages were broken into last night. Yours took the brunt of it, but they were in mine as well."

Struggling to comprehend the news, she took a large sip of coffee and waited for the fog of sleep to clear, before she let anger take over. "Why didn't you wake me up?"

"You were sleeping, and I thought I'd phone the police and then go and wake you, but Officer Rinaldi was in the area, and was dispatched here within minutes to take a look."

At the mention of his name, the officer spoke for the first time. "Good morning, Ma'am. Mr. Sullivan just said he's going to wake you before we go take a look at the cottages."

Sarah nodded in his direction, and turned to Caleb with a hard stare. "Oak Cottages is my responsibility while Gladys is away …"

Before she could continue Caleb cut in with a hard stare of his own, reading her thoughts accurately. "And you're mine! I don't care if your father is having a temper tantrum, I won't let my privacy or yours be invaded so he could prove a point."

Officer Rinaldi looked from Sarah to Caleb. "Your father? Excuse me, Miss, could you maybe explain to me what your father has to do with this?"

Sarah sat, plunking her coffee down in front of her and stared out the window. "I'm not sure, hopefully nothing," she said and continued in a defeated tone of tone, "but probably everything."

"I think you need to explain," Rinaldi requested over a cup of his own.

It took Sarah about thirty minutes to explain the whole story to Rinaldi from finding out about her father's girl on the side, right up to her slashed tires the day before. Rinaldi kept quiet the whole time, taking notes on a little pad, and taking intermittent sips of coffee. When Sarah finally finished she waited for his response.

"Do you know where I can find this Smitty?" Rinaldi enquired.

"No, sorry, I only know him as Smitty, but he's a PI in Savannah. I doubt my father uses him for these kinds of jobs."

"Very well then, let's go see how bad it is."

They got up and started walking toward the cottages. Nothing could prepare Sarah for the chaos that awaited her.

Most of her personal belongings were spread over the grass in front of the cottage. Her underwear lay there in full view of Caleb and officer Rinaldi; the few canvasses that were drying were torn and lay in pieces. Her hand covered her own mouth to stop the gasps fighting to escape.

She walked up the steps into the cottage, hoping it wouldn't be as bad inside as it looked from the outside. It was worse. Her things were spread everywhere, her paints squeezed out of their tubes onto the beautiful floors.

Glancing at Caleb, she asked, "How bad is your cottage?"

He shook his head. "Not this bad, a few things were moved, but nothing was trashed. Not like your place."

"He went too far!" Sarah's blue eyes had turned cold as steel. "This time he went too far."

"Before you go blaming your father, Miss Rothman, can you establish if anything was stolen?" He looked around. "Looks to me like your regular B&E."

"Why only my cottage, why not Caleb's? This is personal." She looked toward Caleb. "This was my father."

Caleb took her hands in his trying to soothe. "Sarah, is anything missing?"

"Nothing that I can tell, it's all just messed up."

"It'll be alright. We'll make this alright." Caleb kissed the top of her head, and that kind affection turned burning rage into a waterfall of tears.

Later, after Rinaldi had filed his report and Caleb had soothed Sarah with tea, she headed out to put her cottage back in order. It took her the better part of the day before she finally sat down with Caleb.

"I have to phone him."

"Your father?"

"Yes, he went too far this time."

"Here use my phone." Caleb handed her his mobile.

She swiftly dialed her home number. It was Saturday, her parents would hopefully be home, it wasn't even lunch time yet.

Her father answered on the first ring. "Rothman."

"You went too far," Sarah said through gritted teeth.

"Sarah," Rothman boomed, "how lovely of you to call. Getting tired of being a chambermaid and a struggling artist?"

"You did this."

"Did what, dear?"

"My car, my cottage, and this time you went too far. You're not going to get me back by sabotaging my life; you're just going to stop me from ever coming back."

The line was quiet for a minute. "What do you mean your car and your cottage?"

"My tires were slashed yesterday, and last night my cottage was broken into and all but destroyed."

Expecting her father to guffaw and deny everything, he instead said in a very somber tone, "Sarah, I've lied to you easily most of my life, I've loved you your entire life, and even though I badly want you to come back to Savannah, I wouldn't do that to you."

Something in his tone made Sarah believe him. "If it wasn't you, who was it?"

She heard her father sigh. "You know if I was behind this my first words would've been it's time for you to come home, and because of that I won't. I want you to believe me that I had nothing to do with this." There was a long pause. "So I'll only say this. Be safe, and take care of yourself. When you're ready, you come back home, but until then, Sarah, please take care of yourself."

Those words made her believe him. He sounded worried, not glum. This wasn't her father's doing. "I will, send my regards to mother."

Before Sarah could ring off her father said, "Wait, Sarah, is C.B. Sullivan still there?"

"Yes."

"Let me speak with him."

Sarah handed Caleb the phone. "He wants to talk to you."

Caleb took the phone with raised brows. "Mr. Rothman?"

"Son, I don't know you, and I am sure you don't want to know me from what Sarah's probably told you of us. That's fine by me. But I need to ask you a favor."

"Yes, sir."

"Take care of her. Something is going on there, which I have nothing to do with. I need you to look out for her."

Caleb turned his back towards Sarah, and answered into the phone, "I will look after her, but I swear to God, if I find out you are behind this, I'll get someone to take care of you."

"Fair enough."

"Goodbye, Mr. Rothman."

"Sullivan." With that the line was dead.

Caleb turned back to Sarah. "Until this is sorted out, I'm staying with you. I don't know if your father is lying, but either way I'm not taking a chance."

Sarah looked at Caleb, knowing if she refused he would just haul her over his shoulders and lock her in cottage. His eyes had that gleam of darkness it had when he was writing.

She simply nodded. "Fair enough."

"What did you make of your dad's words?" Caleb asked.

"It wasn't him. I've heard my dad deny something he did, Caleb. He would have a straight face and deny it cheerfully." She sighed. "He wasn't cheerful, he was worried."

"Who else then?"

"What do you mean who else, I don't know anyone in Blue Hill well enough to make enemies."

"Sarah, I spoke to Rinaldi and he agrees this isn't random, the two incidents within twenty-four hours. This feels personal."

Sarah got up and started pacing. "I've read your books, I'm not stupid, I know this is personal, I just wish I knew why."

"Try, Sarah, think who would be this mad at you?"

Sarah paced deep in thought for a few moments. "Grant? I did leave him practically at the altar and only sent him a letter to explain. He could've found out from my parents where I am, but I doubt he would do this."

"Phone him, at least we can establish if he's in Savannah or not."

"Caleb, what do I say? Remember me, I left you at the altar without an explanation, so have you been to Maine recently with a side trip of slashing tires and vandalizing cottages?"

"If you have to, yes, but we have to get to the bottom of this, and at least we'll know if we can eliminate him, or tell the police we have a lead." He handed her the phone again.

"I can't believe I'm actually doing this," she said as she started dialing Grant's home number.

It was answered after a few short rings. "Go for Grant."

Sarah couldn't help but smile affectionately. She missed her friend. "Hey, it's me."

"Sarah? How are you, where are you? Where the fuck were you on our wedding day?"

Sarah laughed. "Oh, I missed you! Which of those would you like me to answer first? Did you get my letter?"

"All of the above," he said, exasperated, and then added, "I got your letter."

"Grant, I couldn't marry you. You know we were friends, there was never a spark, I couldn't do that to either of us. As to where I am, I am in Maine, overlooking the Mount Desert Narrows."

"You could've told me before the wedding, Sarah."

"I know, and I've wanted to phone you every day since then, but I was afraid you wouldn't be able to forgive me."

"And now you're not afraid anymore?"

"No, I still am, but I needed to ask you something."

"No, I'm not going to marry you, Sarah." A laugh rang out through the room as old friends reconnected.

Grant continued, "I'm planning to travel for the next year, do some soul-searching myself."

"That's wonderful, Grant … makes you realize I did the right thing?"

"Yes, it did. So I'll forgive you this time. What can I do for you?"

"Have you been out of state the past few days?"

"No, why?"

"Not at all?"

"No, Sarah. I can send you the GPS coordinates on my phone to verify. Want to tell me why?"

"I've been having some trouble in Maine, I thought …" her voice trailed off.

"You thought I went psycho groom on you?" Grant let out another booming laugh.

"I know it was stupid, I just had to be sure."

"Well, I've been busy planning my itinerary; I'm leaving next week, first stop South America."

"That sounds exciting, Grant, I hope you enjoy it."

"Me too, take care, Sarah."

"I will." With that she hung up. "This isn't coming from Savannah, Caleb."

"Then we need to be extra careful."

Sarah nodded in agreement.

Chapter 20

THE following morning Sarah did a run through of the cottages. Gladys was due back in that evening and Sarah did a few last minute checks on linen, light bulbs and amenities.

As she opened the door to one of the hidden cottages behind the main house, her blood ran cold. She had felt someone watching her since the break in two days ago, but told herself to ignore it. She couldn't anymore. Fear crawled up her spine like a cold vice grabbing hold of her limbs and numbing her mind. *Run.* That was the only coherent thought she had.

She ran towards Caleb cottage and burst through the door. "They were here."

Caleb got up and moved towards her reading the fear in her eyes. "What do you mean they were here?"

"In one of the cottages behind the house."

"Did you see them?" Caleb took her hand and started dragging her out the door.

"I didn't, but I'll show you." They walked briskly to the cottage in question.

As they entered, Caleb understood exactly what she meant. The bed was unmade; there was half a cup of coffee next to the small kettle on the serving area. The steam was still rising from the shower. Whoever spent the night here had left seconds before Sarah had arrived.

"Sarah, go to the house. Phone Officer Rinaldi and stay there."

"Caleb, be careful." Her knees were shaking and sweat had built on her brow. She had never known a fear as real as this.

Caleb took her face in his hands. "Whoever spent the night here is close by. I want you safe. I'm going to look around to see if I can find them, and I'll be up as soon as possible, but we need the police, Sarah." His green gaze met her blue. "Do you understand?"

"Yes." Sarah nodded.

"Go, and hurry."

Sarah ran towards the main house, bursting through the kitchen door panting with fear still crawling up her spine. As she bent over to take a breath, she heard a movement behind her.

Not knowing how she could be more afraid than she currently was, a fresh wave of panic flushed through her system. She started moving backwards slowly toward the pantry; there were pans and knives in there she could use to defend herself.

As she scanned the kitchen she could see nothing out of place, except for muddy footprints on the floor, besides her own. She took another step backward toward the pantry when suddenly the pantry doors burst open.

Before Sarah could move the cold blade of a knife bit into her throat. "Hello there."

Sarah took a minute to identify the voice. Fighting back fear, she focused on the feel of her attacker behind her.

"I forgot to make the bed."

The voice fell into place, the same shrill taunting voice that had forced doubts of Caleb into her mind in Wilmington.

"Megan," Sarah said on a short breath, careful not to move, afraid of being cut.

"Hello, Sarah," she hissed into Sarah's ear.

"What do you want?" Sarah asked, trying to remain calm. Caleb would come any moment.

"You, of course." Megan laughed a sound that scared Sarah more than the knife to her throat. Megan was enjoying this.

"Alright, what are you going to do with me?" *Keep her talking*, Sarah thought to herself, *the longer she talks the more time Caleb will have to reach me.*

"I told you he killed my sister, and he doesn't love you the way he loved her." She fiddled with the blade, resettling it closer to Sarah's carotid artery. "But I can imagine it would be justice if I killed you."

"Me for Elizabeth?" Sarah asked quietly.

"Like I said, he doesn't love you, but he does like you. He took her from us, now it's time to take something from him."

Sarah thought of all the criminal stories she had read and watched, and decided to play along. "If he doesn't love me, Megan, why would it hurt him for you to kill me?"

Megan pushed the knife tighter against Sarah's throat. "Don't try and get smart."

Sarah made a small nod with her head, knowing that arguing would only get her carotid cut faster. "Tell me about Elizabeth."

The pressure on the knife lessened a little. "She was everything. She was beautiful and smart and I let her have Caleb because I loved her."

"You let her have Caleb?"

"Why, of course. Caleb was in love with me, but when I saw how Elizabeth looked at him, I thought I'd give him to her as a gift."

Realizing how deluded Megan was, Sarah kept quiet, not pointing out that she was twelve at the time and Caleb a senior.

Megan continued wistfully, "It worked, they fell in love, and I could still see Caleb whenever he came over. He would always tell me jokes and listen to me when I talked. But then they moved out. He wanted her for himself. He wouldn't share my sister with me. Then when he was tired of her he killed her."

Sarah couldn't stop the words that escaped her mouth. "It was a car accident, Megan, not murder."

She flinched as the knife was shoved harder against her throat.

"That's what they all say. But I know the truth."

Megan was quiet for a few seconds, as if contemplating if she should just kill Sarah or draw it out a little more. She decided on the latter. She had been building up to this for years; she didn't want it over so soon. Sarah's fear fed her need for power.

"Does he eat potato chips in bed with you?"

"How did you know?" Sarah asked, wondering how long she had been watched by this unstable woman.

"He used to do it with Elizabeth. They never knew, but I would come over and watch them through the windows. I had to make sure he was taking good enough care of Elizabeth." She gave another sinful laugh. "And I had to see if he knew how to use that wonderful body he has."

Sarah kept on scanning the windows for signs of Caleb. The knife was biting into the flesh at her throat and she didn't know how much longer she could keep Megan talking. But she understood something now. Megan was obsessed with her sister and in love with Caleb. For someone that had an unstable mind to begin with, Elizabeth's death would've caused detrimental effects.

"What if I left and never contacted Caleb again?" Sarah asked, grasping at straws.

"But then it wouldn't hurt as much as standing over your grave. And I'll be there to comfort him."

Caleb went through the cottage, hoping something was left behind to indicate who this might be. He phoned Rinaldi directly to find out how far he was.

He picked up on the first ring. "Rinaldi."

"It's Caleb Sullivan, how far out are you?"

"Well, actually I'm in the diner at the moment. Did we have a meeting?"

Fear clawed its way through Caleb's chest. "Sarah didn't phone you?" he said on a deep intake of breath.

"No, why?"

"Get your ass over here now, Rinaldi, whoever is doing this is here." Before Rinaldi could question Caleb, he shouted into the phone, "Now, Rinaldi!"

Caleb sprinted towards the main house, slowing down as he approached the kitchen windows. If Sarah was in there with someone it would be best to keep his approach quiet, maintaining the element of surprise.

The adrenaline pumping through his system didn't dim the fact that he just realized he loved her. Not the kind of infatuation he had for Elizabeth - that was puppy love compared to what he felt for Sarah – but true love. He couldn't let anything happen to her.

He hunched below the kitchen window when he heard voices.

"You're nothing compared to Elizabeth," Megan shouted. "And when you're dead he'll know standing over your grave that he didn't love you. He won't hurt, he'll be relieved."

Chapter 21

MEGAN. The shock hit him like a blow to the heart. This wasn't about Sarah, this was about him. *He* had caused this. It was his fault.

Megan wanted revenge for her sister's death. Instead of waiting for Rinaldi, Caleb approached the kitchen door. He walked in masking his fear with a charming smile.

"Megan, how lovely to see you."

He recognized the look in Megan's eyes as malice and his gaze settled on the carving knife resting on Sarah's throat.

Megan's eyes focused on Caleb. "Caleb," she said hopefully.

"How are you?" Caleb asked, pretending not to be phased at all by the situation in front of him.

"I'm fine, Caleb, but it's time Sarah died," Megan said, not losing focus on her goal.

"Alright, but why exactly?"

Megan fought between her two main motivators - her love for Caleb and her hate towards him for killing her sister. She went with the latter. "Because you killed my sister. You need to lose something you love."

Sarah realized Caleb had no idea how Megan actually felt about him and took the opening to clue him in, hoping he would understand. "But, Megan, Caleb doesn't love me, he loves you. He was telling me in Wilmington how much he loved you, but he didn't think you'd ever forgive him for Elizabeth."

"Shut up," Megan growled and pressed the knife harder, nicking skin.

It only took that moment for Caleb to understand Sarah's message.

"That's true, Megan," he said as he started walking towards her. "I've always loved you, but how could I tell you that when you were still grieving for your sister?"

The pressure of the knife at Sarah's throat lessened; she felt a small trail of blood trickling down her neck. "You did?"

"Of course, but I think we've given it enough time. The time is right for us to start a life together."

Megan wanted to be hopeful, but how could she trust the man that killed sister? "Prove it to me."

"How, Megan? I've yearned for you. Sarah was simply keeping the sheets warm, a little entertainment while I was writing my book. You didn't actually think I felt something for her."

"*You* kill her," Megan said with cold vengeance. She shoved Sarah towards Caleb.

Taking his cue, Caleb grabbed Sarah and pinned her to the counter with her hands behind her back.

Megan closed in, a malice shining in her eyes. "Here, use the knife."

Caleb glanced at the knife. "Megan, you know I don't like blood. Rather fetch me a pan or something heavy from the pantry."

Megan turned, and in that instant Caleb let go of Sarah and wrestled Megan to the floor.

"What are you doing? You're supposed to love me!"

"Yeah, and you're supposed to be sane."

Sarah started sobbing for air, but pushed it back, she had to help Caleb.

"Go find something to tie her up with," he prompted.

Obliging, Sarah rummaged in the pantry and came out with a piece of twine. Caleb swiftly tied Megan's hands behind her back.

"Caleb, don't, please. I love you. I never really blamed you for Elizabeth. Don't do this to us."

He tossed the rope to Sarah. "Tie her feet."

Sarah did as she was told, and pulled the twine just a bit too tight around Megan's ankles, and she responded with, "Ouch!"

"You owe me a set of tires, bitch." Sarah finished the knot and stood back just as officer Rinaldi walked in the door.

He looked at the nick on Sarah's neck, the tear of blood running down her throat, and surveyed the scene, finding Caleb on top of a girl that was tied up. "What the hell is going on?"

"Officer Rinaldi, meet Megan. Her hobbies include spying, slashing tires, B&E and attempting to slit Sarah's throat," Caleb growled.

As Rinaldi bent over Megan to secure her with cuffs, Caleb went to where Sarah sat on the floor sobbing. Without saying a word, he sat down and pulled her into his lap. "I love you."

Sarah heard the words, but relief washed over her for a time as Rinaldi led Megan out the door, saying, "Caleb, I need you both to come and give statements down at the station today still."

Caleb nodded and turned back to Sarah.

She didn't want to accept the words Caleb just gave her. She stood up and felt released. She now knew her father wasn't behind any of it. "Just give me a minute to freshen up, and then we can leave."

"Sarah, can we talk about this?"

"Later, Caleb, now I first need a minute alone so I can pull myself together before we go to the station."

"Fair enough," Caleb said. "I'm sorry, Sarah."

"For what, Caleb? You couldn't know."

He moved towards her and took her hands in his. "For thinking it was your father, for not realizing and, worst of all, for what you had to listen to."

Sarah smiled weakly. "It's over now."

As she closed the bathroom door behind her, Caleb wasn't sure if she meant the situation with Megan or their relationship. He wasn't going to ask her about that now, he'd give her time first, to recover and then he would make her listen to how he felt about her.

The rest of the day was filled with a collection of beady eyed detectives, stale coffee and repeating the story exactly five times before everyone was satisfied enough to let Sarah and Caleb go.

Megan's parents were on their way from Wilmington to offer support and hire a lawyer.

Megan was being charged with Vandalism, Breaking and Entering and Attempted Homicide.

Caleb felt sorry for Megan, but hopefully now her parents would realize that she needed more help than they had offered in the past, that she was mentally ill, not just a little fragile.

When they reached Oak Cottages Gladys was waiting for them in the kitchen. She spotted the weariness and tension they dragged inside with them. "What's wrong?"

Sarah walked to Gladys and was embraced like a mother would a child. She felt the adrenaline drain away and a sinking tiredness creep over her.

"Thank God you're back; I didn't realize how much I needed that."

Gladys looked at Caleb, raising her eyebrows.

"I'll tell you all about it, but right now it would be wonderful if you could help her draw a bath and give her some headache tablets."

Gladys nodded and started fussing and led Sarah up the stairs.

When she returned Caleb had a pot of tea waiting.

"Caleb, that girl is damn near dead on her feet, and silent as a mute. I expect a damn good explanation."

Caleb pulled out a chair for Gladys. He poured her a cup of tea and started right at the beginning. Gladys listened but couldn't quite believe this had all happened under her roof and she wasn't even there to help.

"So all of this is because of Elizabeth's sister Megan."

Caleb nodded. "We first thought it was her father, he had been making threats from his side as well, but now we know better."

"You owe that man an apology, Caleb, especially if you're planning to become part of the family."

"It's that obvious?"

"It is to me," Gladys said. "If I were you, I'd phone the man and tell him what just happened. Even if he is still spitting mad with his daughter, she remains just that."

Caleb agreed, and pulled out his phone. He went back to the dialed numbers of a few days before and located her father's number.

Sarah had never slept that deeply. She remembered vaguely waking in the early hours of the morning, sweating and screaming, before Caleb pulled her close and promised to take care of her. She fell right back to sleep in the crook of his arm.

Now she was slowly drifting out of dreamland and could still feel Caleb's arms around her. She tried to pry herself free without waking him.

"Where are you going?" Caleb muttered.

"Getting up."

"But why?"

"Because it's morning and that's normally what people do in the morning?"

"Not this morning." Caleb pulled her close and slid his hands under the night garment Gladys had borrowed her.

Sarah felt her blood heating even though there was a definite chill in the air.

Caleb abruptly pulled his hand away. "Before I touch you I need to tell you something."

Sarah faced him. "What?"

"I'm in love with you."

"Caleb, don't …"

"Don't you *Caleb don't* me. I love you and you're going to hear it for the rest of your life, so you might as well get used to it."

Sarah closed her eyes and shook her head. Caleb knew it was going to take more than three little words to convince her.

"I've never met anyone as brave as you." He started playing with strands of her hair. "The first time I saw you, you looked utterly perfect and disheveled at the same time. You kept ironing your jeans with your hands. I had this sudden impulse to drag you to my cottage and forget about the book. But I pushed it away. I didn't want to open my heart to you. I was afraid Elizabeth still had the bulk of it."

At Elizabeth's name Sarah looked him in the eye. "I don't want to live in her shadow," she said in a small voice.

"I never expected you to. I told you before, you made room in my heart. I want you to believe it. After we went to Wilmington I realized something, but you were pulling back and I didn't know how to tell you."

"Tell me what?"

"That I never wanted to compare what we have to what I had with Elizabeth, but I've come to realize what I had with her was an infatuation, puppy love, if you like. I will always love her in some way, but what we have is more. I don't know how else to say it. But it's *more*, Sarah. You're more, you mean more."

A tear slid down her cheek. "I don't know what to say."

"Tell me the truth. We've both been treating our time in Blue Hill as the only time we'll have and it doesn't have to be. How do you feel about me?"

Sarah looked down at her hands, drew in a deep breath and looked at Caleb. "I love you too."

With her hair tangled from sleep, her cheeks rosy, without a trace of makeup, to Caleb Sarah had never looked more beautiful. He took her mouth with a fierce hunger and plundered. His hands couldn't work fast enough to get the bed covers off and the night garment out of his way. When his mouth reached flesh he feasted. A joy filled his heart, love and light, and he now understood what that meant. When you truly loved, all your troubles became light.

Sarah could feel the hunger and touched him with the same fervency. They could be more. Through the haze of sleep Sarah realized this was what she was hoping for. She didn't want to greet Caleb when she left in a few days; she wanted a future with him without the shadow of Elizabeth. He had just assuaged her biggest fear.

With the confidence that came from love she reached for him. Their lovemaking was slow and meaningful. Tastes were savored, hearts were touched and they both recognized the love they felt for each other without the doubts and shadows clouding them.

Sarah let out a small giggle as she finally stood up.

"Don't," Caleb muttered again.

"I have to go to the bathroom."

As she walked past the window, she noticed a white blanket of snow had settled on Blue Hill, and stopped to take it in. The snow was still fresh, untrodden. Not yet the muddy slush they would come to hate later that day.

For Sarah it meant a fresh start, a clean slate.

As they descended the stairs together, voices were laughing in the kitchen. Sarah thought it to be Officer Rinaldi doing a follow up, but as she entered the kitchen, she could barely make out the faces of her mother and father as they rushed to her and hugged her.

"Sarah, we were so worried. We're sorry. We love you."

Sarah struggled to tell who said what as they talked and explained at the same time. After a few more hugs and kisses Sarah pulled back, unfamiliar with this level of affection from her parents.

Her father turned to Caleb. "Thank you for phoning us, Mr. Sullivan. And thank you for taking care of her."

Sarah looked toward Caleb and smiled. "You phoned them?"

"They're family, Sarah." He said it as if that meant everything, swiftly putting the past few months of conflict in the past for all of them.

"Thank you."

Her parents looked at her with questioning gazes. "Sarah, could we have a word with you before breakfast?" her mother asked cautiously.

Sarah looked towards Caleb, indicating he could go on ahead without her. She led her parents into the study, closing the door behind them.

"What would you like to talk about?" she asked as she turned to her parents.

"About why you left Savannah," her mother answered.

"About father's affair?" Sarah glanced from her mother to her father, waiting for the reprimand she knew would come.

"Yes," her father answered. He sighed before he continued, "Your leaving caused me and your mother to take stock of our lives, like we haven't in long, long time."

Her mother took her father's hand. "We realized that we'd grown apart, through your father's work and my charities and social obligations, and somewhere we lost sight of the reason we got married."

Her father smiled at her mother with a fondness she had never before witnessed. "Your bravery saved our marriage, Sarah. We started seeing a marriage counselor, I broke off the affair, and we're working through things."

Sarah looked at them, confused. "So all is just forgiven?"

"Of course not, Sarah," her mother said as she moved towards her, taking her hands in her own. "Nothing that took this long to deteriorate can be fixed overnight. However, your father and I have come to realize we both have work to do, it will take time and patience, but we believe that we still love each other and we both want to make it work."

"It was his fault." Sarah accused.

Her mother shook her head. "It was both our faults. I spent all my time planning charities and giving attention to every event I felt needed me, and in time I stopped giving your father any attention."

"Seeing a marriage counselor isn't a blame game, Sarah. We're working through what went wrong and how we can avoid it in future. All we ask of you is to be happy for us. And to believe in us."

Her father turned and kissed her mother, before looking to Sarah for an answer.

She struggled to comprehend all that was just said, but some of it made sense. Her mother always had a cause more important than her daughter and her husband. Maybe she was bit hasty in judging them. "I'm really happy for you and I hope you can work through it."

They hugged again, and Sarah could hardly believe it. The second hug from her parents in one day, after a lifetime of barely touching, and she thought maybe miracles did happen.

As they all sat down to a wonderful breakfast Gladys had prepared, Mr. Rothman raised his glass. "To my daughter, the most stubborn, beautiful, tough and inspiring woman I've ever known. It took us some time to realize this, Sarah, but we'd rather have you butting heads with us and being yourself than being agreeable and wasting away."

Sarah's jaw nearly hit the table. She didn't know what crawled over her father's liver, but she was shocked at his words. She jumped up and grabbed him in a bear hug. "I love you, dad."

They were both so stunned at her use of the word for the first time in their life that they hugged again. Sarah's mother joined the hugging, and couldn't help but laugh when Caleb interrupted with,

"Do you Rothmans ever eat or do you just stand around hugging?"

Everyone laughed and breakfast was enjoyed over comfortable conversation, the first relaxed exchange Sarah had ever had with her parents. Gladys and Caleb could see how much it meant to her. They listened as Gladys explained how much help she was around the cottages and when Caleb applauded her painting, they even promised to stop by the Gallery on their way home.

After a tearful goodbye to her parents without any prompting from them for her to come home, another car pulled up.

Lila's tummy was starting to grow with life; the small bump already caused a slight waddle as Lila moved towards Sarah. "Oh, my God, Mitch told me what happened, he and Rinaldi are friends," she said without pausing for breath. "I was so worried. Are you alright?"

"I am, thank you, just a little shaken up."

"You poor thing, and here I was complaining last night to Mitch about having tried on close to a million wedding dresses not finding the right one, and here you were being held hostage by a crazy person."

"Well, it really wasn't that bad."

Sarah could tell Lila was feeding off the excitement of the whole episode. Obviously something this thrilling hadn't happened in Blue Hill in ages. A thought sprung to mind on how she could distract Lila.

"You say you haven't found a wedding dress yet?"

"No! My tummy isn't that big, but I can't find anything with an A-line in this town. That's the only cut that would hide or at least complement the bump."

"Maybe I can help you with that."

She took Lila's hand and led her to her cottage. After Sarah had laid her own wedding dress down on the bed, she could see Lila's mouth was the shape of an 'O'.

"Sarah, it's beautiful! But where would I find the money to buy it? It looks very expensive."

Sarah laughed. "It was, but if you like it and it fits, see it as an early wedding gift."

After much deliberation and thank you hugs, Lila tried the dress on. The dress wasn't taut over her tummy and would give her a little room for growth; furthermore it looked beautiful on Lila.

"Why on earth would you have a wedding dress lying around?" Lila asked as she started to undress.

"Let's just say I had the right dress, the wrong guy and never made it down the aisle."

"This is wonderful, Sarah, I really don't know how to thank you. Now I have the right guy, the right dress, and I can't wait to walk down the aisle."

A few tears and hugs later, Lila bundled up the dress and headed home.

Caleb sat on his porch and watched the whole scene unfold.

Sarah had just given her wedding dress away. He wondered if she knew that she had finally forgiven her parents and put the past behind her.

Sarah joined him on his porch with a soft smile. "What's on your mind, C.B. Sullivan?"

"That I'm in love with a beautiful, kind-hearted woman, and I'd like to take a walk with her on the beach."

"You do realize it's cold?"

"Of course, that's why we'll layer."

After bundling into several layers along with coats and scarves, they walked down to the beach. They walked in silence for a while, both lost in their own thoughts.

"I enjoyed this morning so much," Sarah said as she picked up a pebble and tossed it into the water.

"I'm glad, I was afraid you'd be mad at me for phoning them."

"Thank you."

"Don't thank me yet, I have another favor to ask."

"Shoot, I'm feeling very favorable at the moment."

"Stay."

"Here?"

"No, stay with me, we could stay in Blue Hill or you could move to Wrightsville Beach with me. You'll paint, I'll write, and somehow we'll manage the four kids running around in the house."

Sarah couldn't contain her laughter. "Four kids?"

"Of course, we need two girls and two boys so we can name them after their grandparents."

"Fair enough," Sarah smiled.

"Is that a yes?"

"Is your name C.B. Sullivan?"

"Yes," Caleb smiled hopefully.

"Then you have your answer." Sarah reached up on her toes with the wind chilling her face. She found warmth and shelter in Caleb's embrace, the wind and cold completely forgotten as their lips met.

Epilogue

THE dress wasn't stifling, it was beautiful. The marriage of silk and lace fit Sarah's body beautifully.

She was standing in the room where she had spent her first night at Oak Cottages, and today she would be getting married here, at the place where she found herself and found Caleb.

It was spring time in Blue Hill; the sky was clear with promise.

This time she couldn't wait to walk down the aisle. Her parents had had such a scare with the whole Megan fiasco that they had put their differences behind them, and embraced Sarah's choices, even her painting.

A year ago Sarah would never had thought her life would've ended up here. Here she was, part-owner in Oak Cottages, Gladys had mentioned the responsibility was becoming too much for her, and Sarah obliged by buying into Oak Cottages.

Caleb's book was being released next week. After their honeymoon in the Caribbean, she would be accompanying Caleb on his book tour.

Sarah looked out the window. The white lawn chairs was filling up with friends and family. The beautiful gazebo overlooked the sound. White orchids, lilies and daisies graced the aisles. A red carpet led from the front door of Oak Cottages to where Caleb stood with Max and Neal looking very handsome.

A knock at the door had her turning her attention back to the room. "Come in."

"Sarah, you have never looked more beautiful."

"Thank you, daddy."

"Are you ready to tie the knot this time?" her father asked earnestly, until a twinkle lit in his eyes. "Otherwise I have a car waiting in the back."

"That won't be necessary; I can't wait to walk down the aisle this time."

"I'm happy for you, darling, and I can see he makes you happy."

"He does."

"Well, come on then." Taking her hand, her father led her down the stairs and paused at the front door. "I don't know how to say this, but I need to say it before giving you away." Her father took a deep breath and reached for her hands. "I know your mother and I failed in raising you. We were so consumed with having the perfect daughter, which you always were, that we never stopped to think what you want. I'm sorry for that. But I can tell you, despite all the wrong we did, I couldn't be prouder of the wonderful woman you have become."

"Oh, daddy." Sarah hugged him.

"No, don't cry now, you'll spoil your face, and ruin your hair if you don't let go." He wiped her tear away with a handkerchief. "Come on, let's get you hitched."

Laughter bubbled from Sarah at her father's comment.

As the doors opened, Salut D'Amour started, played by an expert pianist. Caleb's eyes found hers, and the rest of the world faded away.

Today she would start a new life, a new beginning with a man she mostly understood, but loved even in the times she didn't.

The End

Watch out for the next book in the Sullivan Series

For Justice & Love

When a female firefighter rescues a state prosecutor in the middle of the night the heat is about to rise...

After fleeing an abusive relationship Delta Eckhart plans on starting a new life in a new town. Her only plan is to heal her heart along with her bruises.

Neal Sullivan is a prosecutor for the State of Delaware. He has committed his life to pursuing justice, albeit with a perpetual frown and an aversion to relationships.

When Delta rescues Neal from a broken elevator, the attraction is instant but both Delta and Neal deny it. The heat imminently rises when they discover they are neighbors.

Will Delta be able to heal the wounds of an abusive relationship and open her heart to love again? Can Neal learn that there is a place for love in his life along with the pursuit of Justice?

Will justice or love prevail?

ABOUT THE AUTHOR

Milan Watson is the mother of two little boys and wife to a supportive husband, who doesn't mind doing the dishes when she finds herself lost in a story.

She spends most of her days dreaming up new characters and bringing stories to life, surrounded by her family and her two dogs, Wendy and Duke. She loves creating characters you can identify with and writing stories that will have you laugh, cry and smile at the same time.

You can follow her page on Facebook for new releases:
Milan Watson Author
If you'd like to sign up for her mailing list feel free to send her a
mail at milanwatsonauthor@gmail.com